LOCKED
IN **FEAR**

LOCKED IN FEAR

LIZ COWLEY AND DONOUGH O'BRIEN

Urbane
PUBLICATIONS

urbanepublications.com

First published in Great Britain in 2020 by Urbane Publications Ltd
Unit E3 The Premier Centre Abbey Park Romsey SO51 9DG
Copyright © Liz Cowley & Donough O'Brien, 2020

A CIP catalogue record for this book is available from the British Library.

ISBN 978-1-912666-69-0
MOBI 978-1-912666-70-6

Design and Typeset by Michelle Morgan

Cover by Julie Martin

Printed and bound by 4edge UK

URBANE
urbanepublications.com

"From my own experience as a former prisoner and now as a Prison Chaplain I found *Locked in Fear* an entirely credible story of high drama behind bars. The terrifying 'Big Mack' and his murderous drug accomplices are all too realistic.
The authors write with verve and page-turning excitement".

The Reverend Jonathan Aitken, Prison Chaplain

CHAPTER 1

BIGHTON, HAMPSHIRE

'BENNY!'

Everything had been going so well, until the dog limped into the house whimpering and covered in blood.

Up to that moment Pam Marshal had felt surprisingly upbeat – despite the fact that she was becoming immobilised by Parkinson's Disease and these days was mostly confined to a wheelchair. She had reflected how lucky she was to have a husband like Robin who had retired early from the police force to look after her and suggested moving to the country, both decisions that initially worried her considerably. But to her surprise and delight, he had thoroughly embraced a quiet life near an attractive village called Bighton, near Winchester, in Hampshire. Nor was it the too-quiet life she had feared it would be, with several new friends and visitors and delightful neighbours.

She had never imagined for a minute that Robin would embrace a whole new hobby – let alone gardening – which now took up a large part of his time every day. And it was a pleasant daily ritual to manoeuvre her new Cirrus Plus electric wheelchair around the specially paved paths along the borders that had replaced the gravel ones as soon as they had moved in, gravel being a wheelchair's worst enemy.

Nor had she ever visualized owning a dog – 'Ben' – a retired police Alsatian, or one with such a delightful nature, touchingly dividing his time between her and Robin. Neither of them had ever wanted a dog in London, not with the wretched business of having to scoop up excrement from the pavements. But now neither of them could imagine life without one.

So much had changed since they had come to Hampshire – even Robin's appearance. She had only just got used to him sporting a beard, and often wearing dark glasses – even when it wasn't sunny – and almost always seeing him in informal clothes – obviously protecting his identity as many retired police officers did. And she had been amazed and touched by his attention to the house and the time he had put into the renovation plans on her behalf.

Everything both outside and inside had been adapted to make her life easier – a bedroom for the two of them downstairs with an adjoining shower room, ramps at every doorway, two more bedrooms upstairs for when their two sons and granddaughter or friends came to stay, and a large and specially adapted kitchen with everything in easy reach – not least the vases that she filled each week through the summer with flowers that Robin proudly brought in from outside.

She had been watching the television with the Wimbledon final between Andy Murray and Novak Djokovic, wishing that Robin liked tennis as much as she did but delighted he enjoyed his days outside, and turning up the volume to drown out the sound of the mower.

It was a thrilling match, the most exciting she had ever watched. Halfway through she had glanced out of the window and seen a tall stranger approaching Robin at the far end of the lawn, immediately assuming it must be the chap who was coming to help him to clear the shed. About time too, she thought. Six months after moving in it was still full of things from their London house that neither they, their sons or any of their friends wanted, mostly what people now deprecatingly called 'brown furniture'.

An hour later, and with a great victory for Murray, she had steered her chair towards the kitchen to start preparing supper – always a pleasant ritual with the home-grown vegetables that Robin brought in regularly. Life was still good, she thought to herself.

It was at that precise moment when Ben, their beloved Alsatian appeared –whimpering, slumping at her feet and bleeding heavily.

'Benny!' She stretched out a hand to him as a wave of shock coursed through her. What on earth had happened? And where was Robin?

'BEN, STAY!'

Her heart pounding, she pushed the button on the Wander Alert always worn around her neck, scooped up the phone and drove her chair into the garden and towards the shed. The two minutes to get there felt like two hours.

To her horror, there was Robin lying on the floor – battered, bloodied and unconscious. Her hand shaking, she dialled 999, aware of her heartbeat now going through the roof.

'Emergency. Which service?'

'Ambulance! And police, as fast as you can!'

||||||

That's the last job we'll ever give that idiot Rory. Great big fella sent to do a pensioner and he gets bitten by a bloody dog, doesn't finish the job and then whines to my boys about needing injections. Christ Jesus! That's the problem of being stuck in here and not able to do the job yourself.

CHAPTER 2

PUTNEY COMMON, LONDON

Alice Diamond just had time to check her computer before seeing her next patient, and was delighted to find a message from Jean-Michel to say that he was coming to London – the charming Frenchman she had met on a recent clay shooting trip in Bordeaux, and the first man she had been strongly attracted to since splitting up with her boyfriend John three years ago. She reflected that taking up a whole new hobby might turn out to be a good decision in more ways than one, though reminding herself that it was early days.

Losing John had been tough. And it had been made tougher still by the avalanche of publicity surrounding her simultaneous, albeit very brief, relationship with David Hammond whom to her unimaginable horror turned out to be a serial killer. Her face had been splashed all over the papers along with his, and the shame and humiliation had been almost unbearable, similarly the damage to her career.

But at last she was moving on again, really moving on, once more involved with police work as a psychologist and simultaneously running her private practice on Putney Common. The mental scars had at least subsided, and so too had the physical ones from when Hammond had so viciously attacked her. And though not vain she was hugely relieved, specially in a world where appearance mattered so much more than it should. She only had to glance at the magazines in her waiting room to see that. Thousands of impossibly beautiful (though no doubt retouched) faces stared out of the pages each month. And the models were all so tall, a good eight inches more than she was, although being relatively short had never bothered her. Though it sometimes seemed to faze her clients – at least initially – as if mental strength were reflected by physical prowess. Perhaps when treating vulnerable people, it helped if you didn't look vulnerable yourself. But that was the least of her worries these days.

Now thirty-four, these days she often remembered the phrase 'Physician, heal thyself ', and felt she had done just that, allowing that difficult feat to give her pride. Her deep blue eyes, so often described as violet, now looked out far more positively that they had in years, and now there was the pleasant prospect of seeing Jean-Michel again. Things felt good.

Her mood was further enhanced in the hour ahead with her patient Ruth Isaacs. It was wonderful to witness the steady progress she was making since they had first met over a year ago. Ruth was now even able to take a bus to her practice on Putney Common rather than rather than come in a taxi – another huge milestone on her patient's road to recovery.

She thought back to the court case when she had given psychological evidence in court at Ruth's trial – Ruth being in no fit state to do so other than by video link – and when she had painstakingly explained to an astonished courtroom the numerous symptoms of Compulsive Obsessive Disorder that her patient had suffered untreated for years, and which had ultimately led to the death of her husband Leon in a fatal fall down the stairs of their Finchley home.

So much has changed since then, not least Ruth's appearance. Her face looked infinitely less strained then it once was, and today even sported a touch of make-up. And her hands, which were once red raw from endless washing, looked ten times smoother.

Better still, her patient was at last able to shake hands with her, no longer obsessed with picking up germs from other people. Even her once thin red hair had thickened noticeably, no longer pulled out in times of stress, or more likely, as a result of trichotomania.

Alice had never come across such a severe case of OCD before, let alone one that had led to a murder enquiry and encompassed so many different symptoms: fear of causing explosions or fire when cooking which meant Ruth habitually ordered takeaway food and even served that on disposable paper plates. Fear of germs which meant she was constantly cleaning and polishing and changed the family's bed linen every single day. Terrified of eating out or being in any public places and breathing the same air as other people, let alone in a doctor's surgery where contamination was more likely. And totally unable to travel by public transport, fearful of holding on to germ-infested escalator handrails and standing in crowded trains or lifts, inhaling other people's breath.

She remembered the shocked faces of the jury only too well. Wide eyes, open mouths, heads shaking in utter incredulity as she spoke, all the time fearful that her words might not be believed, or sufficiently enough to save Ruth from a protracted prison sentence, or her sons from going into care. She had been further worried by her former notoriety as the short-term girlfriend of David Hammond, the now dead serial killer – if they made that connection – just as much as by the unusual features of this case.

She knew that her audience would have some knowledge of Ruth's disorder, possibly of people unwilling to allow tradespeople to use the loo, having to carry out certain rituals every day and maybe fearful of strange places or faces. But would they believe her evidence in such an unusually advanced case?

Thank God, they did. Better still, several prominent people had 'come out' admitting the disorder, including the mother of a prominent Minister. The Sunday newspapers were full of it.

Ruth had escaped prison in the court case but faced a long struggle to escape the prison of her own mind, and it was one of the greatest challenges that Alice had ever faced, even with her years of working on complex police cases and with hugely damaged minds.

On the day of the accident Ruth's two teenage sons were about to be driven to Heathrow airport by her husband Leon for a greatly anticipated school ski trip to Switzerland – no doubt all the more longed-for because of their mother's daily obsessions – and they had strict instructions to pack their suitcases downstairs in the hall in case they scuffed them against the newly-painted white woodwork on the staircase. Long irritated and frustrated by their mother's numerous obsessions, both boys – in their excitement – had uncharacteristically disobeyed her and the worst had happened, with scuff marks in several places along the skirting boards, and even a tear in the wallpaper above them.

According to her two sons, Tobias and Seth, she had sat at the top of the stairs in uncontrollable floods of tears, keening and rocking herself backwards and forwards as their father tried to console her for about fifteen minutes, eventually realising that if he stayed with her any longer the boys would miss the plane and the hugely anticipated school trip – a much-needed escape from their overly-controlled home environment.

Sitting beside her at the top of the stairs he had then stood up to leave, turning to her one last time to say he would be back as soon as possible, at which point she had sprung to her feet in fury and pushed him with a violent shove – sending him flying backwards down the staircase and landing headfirst on the marble floor of the hall. It was left to the traumatized boys to phone 999 for an ambulance as the pool of blood spread around their father's head and the wailing at the top of the stairs reached a new crescendo.

This tragedy marked the beginning of a protracted enquiry in which Alice was involved, and a complex court case at which she testified – and where Ruth was eventually acquitted due to her spiralling – and until the accident – untreated mental obsessions. The court had been astonished by her sons' evidence and even more than by her own.

Ruth had gradually opened up over the months of counselling, and Alice could at last begin to glimpse the woman she used to be, though still unable – frustratingly – to pinpoint precisely what had tipped her patient into an uncontrollable avalanche of obsessions.

'Can you think of anything, anything at all that might have started this?' was a question that she had asked Ruth many times. She had explored a number of avenues – painful childhood experiences, incidents of trauma and abuse, parents with similar anxieties, stressful events, lack of serotonin. But she was still unable to identify the exact trigger of Ruth's obsessive behaviour, though suspecting that it may have had something to do with her husband's successful career and an overwhelming feeling of being isolated and left behind. While he controlled extensive business interests – the one thing she could control was her home environment, as she clearly had for years and to an obsessive degree.

'Did you ever fear your husband might leave you?' Alice had asked her directly some time ago.

'No, not really. But I was afraid of that, especially once.'

'And when was that?'

'When he hired a new PA at his office and he told me that he saw her eating a baguette at her desk in the lunch hour and dropping crumbs all over the carpet – and herself. He said it almost made him fall in love with her on the spot – noticing she didn't give a damn about the mess. As, of course, I would have done.'

Alice paused. 'But you don't think it came to anything?'

'What? Him and the girl?'

'Yes.'

'No, I don't think so. But it certainly made me feel less secure and more out of control, and that probably made things worse.'

'I'm surprised that didn't prompt you to seek help.'

'It did, but I didn't dare to. As you know, I was initially terrified of seeing you. It was only because the court made me.'

Just after Ruth had left, her long-term assistant Maggie knocked on the door.

'Come in.'

Maggie entered, holding the phone.

'Sorry to interrupt you, but it's Robin Marshal's son Tim on the line. He called a few minutes ago and I asked him to call back. He says it's really urgent.'

Robin Marshal, formerly Detective Inspector Marshal, her old friend and many times colleague on police work. Something serious must have happened for his son to call – and in working hours. Or why wouldn't Robin have called himself? She reached for the phone, suddenly alarmed.

'Hi Tim, it's me.'

'Hi, Alice. Look, I'm afraid I've got bad news. Dad's been rushed to hospital and he's in a pretty bad way. It's touch and go, I'm afraid.'

Alice was stunned into silence.

'Alice, you still there?'

'Yes, what happened?'

'You know he was always fearful of reprisals?'

'Yes.'

Alice knew only too well. She had never needed to ask him why he had changed his appearance so radically since his retirement from the police force, even growing a beard and often donning dark glasses, furthermore moving to the country and a complete change of lifestyle. It certainly wasn't *just* to look after his wife.

'It looks as if his fears were well-founded,' said Tim. 'He's been attacked – and seriously. And he's now in Winchester Hospital in a private room under police guard, and with a changed name.'

'My God!' Alice pictured Robin with horror.

'But you'll be allowed to see him. I've given the police and relevant hospital staff your name and credentials. Got a pen handy?'

'Sure.'

'I'll give you the number and the names at reception to ask for. And if you can, see him as soon as possible. And bring some ID.'

'Of course.'

Dear Robin – the man who had been her constant supporter, indeed her salvation three years ago when she had been briefly involved with that notorious serial killer and he had supported her so loyally, not only during the case, but ever since. Hating to cancel appointments, especially at short notice, Alice had no choice.

'Tim, I'll come first thing tomorrow. I'll call when I'm on my way.'

CHAPTER 3

PUTNEY

Alice phoned the hospital as soon as Ruth had left and arranged to visit Robin the next morning, keeping her mobile in her pocket for the rest of the day. But only one person called, in the evening, and it was not Robin's son. It was her old friend Liz who had introduced her to John, her last serious boyfriend. Things had come to an abrupt halt between her and Liz after the scandal broke about her simultaneous, albeit very brief, relationship with the serial killer David Hammond – which saddened Alice greatly. But at last they were back in touch to her great relief, though with a lot of catching up to do. Alice still hoped their relationship could one day return to what it once was, and Liz's voice brought fresh hope that it would.

'Hi, it's me. Just wondered what you'd been up to.'

Alice decided not to mention the crisis about Robin, keeping the talk light.

'Actually, I've just got back from France. From a shooting trip.'

'Shooting? Gosh, I didn't know you were into that!'

'Nor did I until quite recently. A friend got me into it and I really enjoyed it.'

'What, watching it?'

'No, *doing* it.'

'Good Lord. You never cease to amaze me! What do you shoot at? Pheasants?'

'No, just clay pigeons. Anyway, I started to take lessons and found I was quite good at it. So I bought a gun, a cheap one and nice and light, and joined a women's team. One thing we do is to go off every other year to a competition in France. It's called the 'Coupe des Nations' and used to be men only. But now there's a women's team on each side. We're called the 'Swallows', and the French girls the 'Amazons' – you know, after Arthur Ransome.'

'Gosh, I'm *really* out of touch! You must be bloody good to take part in competitions.'

'Hardly. But good enough not to make a total fool of myself. And the people you meet are great. In fact, I've just met a really nice guy, one of the French. First decent chap I've met in ages.'

'Oh, seems I'm calling at the wrong time.'

Alice thought her anxiety about Robin had shown in her voice. 'Why?'

'Well, I met up with John a few days ago and I got the strong impression he wanted to see you again. He's not getting on too well with his girlfriend and he asked me if you were hitched up with anyone. I said I didn't really know and was a bit out of touch. So, what do I tell him?'

Alice paused.

'I'm not sure. And guys can't just jump from one girl to another. Or at least they shouldn't. That's insulting to both of them. And nor can you go back to the past just like that. Too much water under the bridge.'

It was three years since she'd seen him, after that avalanche of lurid publicity surrounding the Hammond case, with John hounded by the media as well as his family. It was still painful even after all this time remembering how he had finally walked out on her at the local Starbucks in Putney, never to get in touch again.

'Let me think about it, and I'll call you.'

'Well, don't make it too long. John's an attractive man.'

'I know, so he won't find any trouble finding someone else.'

'But not like you. You're a one-off, and he knows it.'

'I'd like to see him again,' said Alice, 'but it took me ages to recover, and I'm not sure I could stand being grilled all over again.'

'I don't think he'd do that. Not after all this time.'

'I'm afraid I do. And his parents wouldn't be all that happy either.'

'At least, think about it. You two had such a good thing going and it's pretty clear that neither of you have found anyone as remotely compatible since.'

Alice was thinking about it, remembering their good times together, and wondering if they could ever happen again, simultaneously thinking about Jean-Michel.

'Look, I'll phone you after I've seen the chap from France.'

'Okay.' Liz sounded disappointed.

'Frankly Liz, if he *really* loved me he'd have been in touch before. And three years is a hell of a long time, and time changes things.'

'And sometimes for the better,' said Liz.

Alice decided to change the subject.

'Anyway, how are you and Derek?'

'Pretty good. Although we still haven't had any luck with IVF. Third time unlucky. And I'm not sure we can afford another failure.'

For the next five minutes Alice encouraged her with what she knew about the latest advances in IVF procedures, surprised that Liz hadn't read about them in the papers. And relieved that she didn't mention John again before ringing off.

How ironic thought Alice as she put away the mobile. Just when you meet a really lovely man, another one comes back out of the woodwork to haunt you.

That night she found it hard to sleep, worrying about Robin and thinking about John and that tumultuous period four years ago. The media had been terrible, of course. All those headlines like 'PSYCHO LOVER', 'SEX ROMPS WITH SUSPECT' and 'COP DOC IN SEXFEST'. So humiliating. And she'd only been out with him three times.

But then, after Hammond's trial and death, that journalist Sarah Shaw had decided that Alice was much more a victim, and what's more, something of a heroine. Her four-page exposé in the *Daily Mail* changed everything. *ALICE DIAMOND, THE TRUTH* had focussed on what a terrible time she'd had and how she had helped to catch the serial killer.

In her desk Alice had a big file, full of kind letters from relatives of his victims. Sheila Corcoran, whose husband had been shot in a Belfast swimming pool, now sent Alice regular Christmas cards from her new home in Melbourne. More cards would come from Lady Hewitt, the widow of the old General gunned down in St James's, and even from the former Home Secretary, who still missed his old political friend James Lonsdale – strangled in Chelsea.

In fact, Christmas brought envelopes with all sorts of foreign stamps. From Poland from Agniezska, now with a completely unpronounceable surname, whose former fiancé had been shot to death on the A1. Each year there was one from Italy, a Vogue Italia card from Katarina, with a scribbled '*I'm glad you got the bastard*', and then one from America, from some people called the Murphys in Chicago.

The first year after the scandal, when she went to visit her father in France, she had been visited by another widow, Viviane Bertrand, and also by the top detective in Quissac who had brought her champagne. They too sent cards. And she even got one from Harry, the son of David Hammond, the killer.

Sarah Shaw's intervention had been beneficial in two ways. First she had become a friend of Alice's. And second, her sympathetic piece had ensured that Alice had become well-known in a positive way attracting more private patients, compensating for her drop-off in Scotland Yard work.

After an hour, Alice was tired enough to nod off.

CHAPTER 4

WINCHESTER HOSPITAL

Seeing Robin Marshal in hospital the next morning had been a shock – ashen-faced, with an oxygen mask, eyes closed, and still unconscious. She could do little more than sit beside the bed holding his hand and hoping he might be aware of her. But there was no reaction, none at all.

She thought back to the time, three years ago, when she had been in hospital after David Hammond had tried to kill her, and when Robin had come to see her regularly – among her very few visitors. She owed him this visit – and more of them, even if it meant more cancelled appointments or a complete break for a while.

Both Robin's sons were at his bedside on arrival, but they both left for an hour so she could be with him alone, and when that time was up she found the older one, Tim, sitting outside the ward with two policemen.

'Thanks again for coming,' he said, getting up from his chair, 'and at such short notice. We really appreciate it, as does Mum. Jamie's had to go to work. And I'm really sorry if you've had to cancel appointments.'

'Don't worry about that,' replied Alice. 'I think we've all got enough to worry about already. In fact, I think it might be a good idea to take a bit of time off work so I can see him more often. And your mother, too.'

'That's really kind, but you don't have to. Jamie and I are both taking time off work to keep an eye on him and Mum – and we've arranged for a full-time carer for her so we can be here more often. Perhaps the best thing to do is to call you if anything changes. The good news is they're cautiously optimistic he's going to pull through.'

Alice breathed a sigh of relief. 'Thank God for that.' She suddenly felt tears welling up in her eyes, and rummaged in her bag for a tissue.

'I'm sorry,' she apologised, dabbing at her cheeks.

'Don't be.'

As they were sitting there, a man stopped to talk to the uniformed policemen sitting outside and then entered the room. He proffered a warrant card.

'Hello. I'm Detective Sergeant Alan Rodgers, Hampshire CID.'

Tim showed his own card and shook his hand. 'I'm Tim Marshal, his son, with the Met, and this is Dr Alice Diamond, a very good friend of his.'

The detective nodded, and then looked carefully at Alice.

I'll bet he remembers the Hammond furore, she thought with embarrassment.

'Good to meet you.' He stretched out his hand before turning to Tim, 'I'm really sorry about your father. We've met him – he made contact with us when he retired down here, although he said he kept police work much to himself.

Anyway, this is what we know so far. Apparently he was expecting someone to come and help him move some stuff in the garage. A friend of a friend. That genuine person was delayed and I suppose Marshal must have assumed the fellow who turned up was the helper.

As soon as they got to the garage, Marshal was attacked and stabbed. But luckily his dog intervened, and the man got bitten and disappeared.

We checked Mr Marshal for DNA, and also sedated the dog

and got it to the vet, where our forensics people managed to find traces of blood, hair and clothing in its teeth and jaw. That's being analysed now.

We've not found the weapon, but indications point to a big knife of some sort.'

He paused.

'Do you have any idea why this might have happened?'

Tim cleared his throat.

'Well, I know my dad was a bit worried about retiring early, concerned that many of the people he'd helped put away might still be active. He'd even changed his appearance and kept strictly out of the limelight – not least to look after Mum. As you know, she's far from well. So, while it might *look* like a botched burglary, there's a chance it's revenge.'

After some discussion about possible motives, Rodgers took down their contact details and promised to keep in touch about any progress.

Alice then spent the rest of the day with Robin's wife at home in Bighton, which was almost more difficult than visiting the hospital. Pam already knew from her sons that the doctors thought there was a good likelihood that Robin would pull through, and Alice returned to that assessment several times in their conversation. What the doctors had not said, of course, was the state Robin would be in if and when he did pull through – and she knew all too well what must be going through Pam's mind.

Halfway through the afternoon, Pam asked Alice if she would stay to supper – an invitation she accepted, though not a bed for the night. Ruth Isaacs was coming to see her at nine o'clock the next morning, and having barely slept a wink the night before, she needed her own bed. She had never found it easy to sleep in strange ones, particularly if she was worried about something or someone, and especially someone she liked as much as Robin.

Returning home at ten o'clock that evening, Alice's mood was lifted by an email from Jean-Michel to say that he'd be coming to London in three weeks time, and inviting her to dinner. But she couldn't believe the restaurant he proposed going to – Nobu – the very same one that David Hammond had taken her to on their first date. The coincidence was somehow freaky. Furthermore, she was frightened that someone there would recognize her and remember the scandal in the papers – maybe that waitress who had blabbed to the press.

But how could she wriggle out of it? Say she didn't like Japanese food? She couldn't bear the risk of being under public scrutiny again, particularly as she knew she had a memorable face with her dark short hair, pale skin and unusually blue eyes. But it sounded so pathetic, so unadventurous, to write off the food of a whole country.

Tell him that it was ludicrously expensive last time she went there, and suggest somewhere else? No, he could probably, no almost certainly, afford it – and would say so.

She eventually decided to tell him that the last time she went there had been a disaster; not the food, but the company of her date, and that she didn't want to be reminded of it. It was the best excuse she could think of, but it might not be an auspicious start.

She was heartily relieved when he replied to her email the next day.

'Fine, let's make it the Ritz, where I'm staying. I'll be in the Rivoli Bar at 7:30 on the 21st May. Okay? J-M.'

She replied to the email straight away. *'The Ritz - lovely! Look forward to seeing you. Best, Alice.'*

CHAPTER 5

KENT

Rory was staring through the windscreen of the Range-Rover, unfamiliar with the scenery. But then he was pretty unfamiliar with the whole of southern England. His patch was the Midlands and the North, or his native Scotland.

'How far is the doctor?' he asked his companions, anxiously. After several days in hiding, his hand was now beginning to hurt badly. It had definitely swollen up and part of it was an unpleasant red and purple colour. He knew enough about infection to realize that sepsis, or that longer word he couldn't remember, was a real danger.

That bastard dog! Nobody had mentioned a dog – and a big one.

'Not long now, mate,' said the driver, now quite irritated by his passenger. 'He lives on the other side of that golf course over to the left. We'll be there in ten minutes. But before we get there, I need to stop and stretch my legs and have a fag. And you can smoke, if you like. When we get there, the doc certainly won't allow it.'

He slowed the big vehicle and pulled into a little lane flanked by thick trees, then stopped and switched off.

Rory climbed slowly down, with difficulty because of his wounded hand. The driver came round the front of the Range-Rover, apparently fumbling for cigarettes.

But what he pulled from his pocket was not a packet, but a large black pistol from which he fired one shot into the top of Rory's head.

CHAPTER 6

PUTNEY

As the days passed, the news about Robin grew better. The knife wounds were healing slowly, luckily there were no signs of infection and at last he was talking again. Alice tried to visit him in hospital every three days or so, slipping away from her practice at about four in the afternoon and getting on to the Kingston by-pass and the A3 before the rush hour traffic. But it still took an hour with all the frustrating speed limits. After a couple of hours at the bedside, she was sometimes able to drop in on an anxious Pam. Driving down the twisting, narrow country lanes to Bighton, took at least half an hour from the hospital, and the diversion meant that she was always pretty tired when she arrived back in London.

Robin proved to be hazy about the attempt on his life, and was still shocked by his own uncharacteristic and casual assumption – which he now remembered only too well – that the stranger was the man supposed to help him clear the garage. How could he – as a senior detective, albeit retired – not have known better, and not asked for some ID?

He remembered the first knife thrust and then trying to fight back, and had no doubt that it was Benny, their dog, who had saved his life, launching himself fearlessly and repeatedly at his attacker. Indeed the stranger's screams and Benny's furious growls still rang clearly in his ears. He knew some people were afraid of dogs, and especially Alsatians, and luckily this man seemed to be one of them, desperately turning from Robin to slash at Benny with his knife.

Now sitting up in bed, Robin was effusive about his dog's loyalty and bravery and was delighted to hear that his pet, too, was on the mend. Alice had smiled to notice two photographs by his bed – one of Pam, the other of Benny.

Robin was now taking both a personal and professional interest in how the Hampshire police were getting on. They, in turn, were also making sure they made every last effort. After all, among their stabbing victims, a former Detective Inspector was unheard of. But progress was slow. They were still waiting for the forensics test results from any DNA found on Robin, the dog, and the crime scene and its surroundings.

The police searching the village and the verges and ditches for the weapon attracted considerable attention among the locals, and especially children. But the protracted search turned up nothing. Bighton itself was a quiet village, and nobody there had noticed anyone acting strangely. The detectives began to think that the efficient escape of an injured man pointed not only to an accomplice, but almost certainly a getaway car. The idea of a burglary gone wrong was looking increasingly unlikely, but Robin, his sons and Alice were all beginning to think that the investigation might reach a dead end.

In the meantime, Alice's workload had piled up, partly because of her voluntary absences to see Robin. She had persuaded some of her patients to come at eight-thirty in the morning which had eased the pressure a bit, although it still made for very full days.

But good news came after two weeks. Robin had been told he could go home in a few days, and the carer had agreed to look after both him and Pam after accepting a considerable hike in her wages, thankfully covered by Robin's insurance.

And now Alice had received more good news in the form of an email confirming her date with Jean-Michel, to which she began to look forward with great anticipation. She felt she could do with some excitement. Dealing with patients one after another, many of them depressed, could get somewhat dispiriting for *her* at times – despite her training in staying professionally detached – and the visits to see Robin and Pam, at least the early ones, had not exactly raised her spirits.

She felt an evening at the Ritz was just what she needed, especially with such an amusing and attractive man.

CHAPTER 7

THE RITZ HOTEL, LONDON

The promising evening had turned into a nightmare, and Alice felt almost tearful in the taxi back to Putney. It had all started so well, with a glass of champagne in the elegant Rivoli Bar as she and Jean-Michel chatted so easily to each other, just as they had in France. There was such a wicked twinkle in those dark brown eyes, and his enthusiasm for life was wonderfully uplifting after seeing two patients with depression that afternoon.

Liking him the moment they met in Bordeaux, she began to do so even more as he told her about his quirky hobbies – not least collecting everything from antique guns to coffee pots, and buttons to model soldiers – which apparently filled his chateau in the Loire and his Paris apartment. Alice was to hear – to her amazement – that he had collected a complete model army of soldiers to re-enact Napoleon's battles – over 2,000 of them – only for him to lose half of them to his ex-wife in their difficult divorce of five years ago. *A completely new take on battle casualties*, she thought.

'Revenge!' laughed Jean-Michel. 'Although *she* left *me*. And she's probably chucked them all out by now! C'est la vie,' he sighed.

It was a vast relief to her that he didn't seem to connect her name with the David Hammond court case, even though it had been widely publicised in France where her father lived, and where she had stayed until the publicity began to subside.

The evening had gone wonderfully well until they were ushered to their table in the magnificent neo-classical Ritz Restaurant.

Minutes later, they were both looking at the menu when Alice glanced up to see who was being shown to the table next to theirs.

To her horror, it was John, her ex-boyfriend, with whom she'd fallen out so acrimoniously three years before, accompanied by a stunning and statuesque redhead.

John had not acknowledged her, though he had certainly noticed her – Alice was quite sure of that. There could be no other reason for him to ask the Maitre d' so quickly if they could be moved to another table nearer the windows overlooking the park.

At once her mood fell – and visibly, to the point where Jean-Michel asked if there was anything wrong.

She had eventually admitted that the man about to sit down was someone she used to go out with, but had fallen out with some time ago, at which point he had commented wryly that she seemed to have rather a lot of people in her life she'd quarrelled with – including the imaginary man at the Nobu. Not a great start.

The evening was wrecked before it was even halfway through. Try as she might, Alice found it impossible to relax and enjoy Jean-Michel's company as much as she had in France or in the Rivoli Bar just minutes before.

Repeatedly she found herself wondering whether she should tell Jean-Michel about the David Hammond case, at one point almost doing so after too much wine, then deciding against that. And all through dinner, she had not been able to resist glancing at John from time to time and remembering the good times.

Being petite, she had never been able to drink much, let alone at least a third of their second bottle of wine. Furthermore, seeing John had made her lose her appetite; with an embarrassing amount of the main course left on her plate – and absolutely no interest in dessert which disappointed Jean-Michel.

'Quel dommage! Their desserts are famous!'

It was almost a relief to climb into the taxi for the miserable journey back home, not remotely confident that Jean-Michel would get in touch again. He'd told her he'd call her, but Alice was almost certain she'd blown it. Should she have taken the risk of telling him about her past? Surely a psychologist should have been able to work that out, she told herself, but try as she might, she couldn't.

Such a nice man, she thought. What a shame.

||||||

'So, what do you think?' John had asked, looking around the restaurant.

'What of?'

'Well, here, the Ritz.'

Susannah had hardly mentioned the magnificent meal, let alone the stunning setting of the Ritz Restaurant – almost as if she hadn't noticed them.

If only she could see beyond herself, he thought – something he hadn't noticed at first, but certainly did now. The past two hours had really been an eye-opener.

In fact, The Ritz was as stylish as ever, even more so since its recent refurbishment. All Fabergé opulence, with its ornate cornices, gilded details and heavy curtains framing the vast windows. And the food was superb – as it should have been at those astronomic prices, he thought somewhat ruefully.

Susannah had chosen oysters and then Beef Wellington with Périgord truffles – almost certainly the most expensive dishes on the menu – and then left half, without as much as a comment. Nor had he liked what she said nearing the end of the meal.

'So where's my *real* present?'

John was astonished. 'I thought this *was* the present,' he said looking around.

'What, this meal? Don't be ridiculous! Presents are things you open and keep, not things you share like dinners out. Things that show some *real* thought, and reflect the other person. At least that was always what I was brought up to think.'

Not for the first time he wondered about her parents, relieved that they lived in Monaco as tax exiles and that he'd never met them. He said nothing, suddenly wondering why he'd ever got involved with this girl – and thinking about Alice. Yes, Susannah was beautiful. Almost as tall as him, with incredible green eyes and a mane of red hair. But what else was there when he really thought about it? And why hadn't he ever noticed that before? Well, he was certainly noticing now.

'And what was all that palaver about changing our table?' she asked. 'At least the couple on the next table were quite glamorous, not in their dotage like most people here.'

'I told you,' said John warily, deciding that this was not the time to explain about Alice. Perhaps a little white lie?

'I fell out with that man some time ago – a business deal that fell through because of him. And I didn't want to spend the evening sitting next to him, or even acknowledge him. And I'm equally sure he didn't want to spend it sitting next to me.'

'He can't be that awful to have a girlfriend like that. Did you notice her eyes? Quite amazing! Almost violet.'

'No, can't say I did,' he lied.

'Probably contact lenses. Nobody has eyes like that.'

John flinched.

Characteristically, she didn't ask what the business deal was and why it fell through. Her mind soon wandered off whenever he mentioned business, those green eyes glazing over. It was something he used to find amusing – and even charming – but not lately, and not now. It had been enough to sport a beautiful girl on his arm, but it wasn't any longer. And when he thought about it, what did she really have to say for herself that wasn't *about* herself?

And what she said in the car on the way back was the final straw.

'I tell you what would have made a *really* nice present. *Staying* at the Ritz overnight, and then wandering down Bond Street in the morning to find something really meaningful – like a ring.'

John was stunned. Even coming from Susannah, that shook him. And did she mean an *engagement* ring? That was the last thing on his mind. He suddenly dreaded being in bed with her when they got home. Thank God he had an excuse to get out of that.

|||||

'John, are you deaf? I said I …'

'I know what you said. But if you don't mind, I'd like a bit of hush. It's not you doing the driving.'

To his profound relief, she complied – until five minutes later.

'Why are we going this way? And not to your place?'

'You've probably forgotten, but I've got a really big presentation tomorrow and I need to get up really early in the morning. And if you don't mind, I need to sleep alone.'

Susannah groaned. 'Well, what a romantic birthday *this* has turned out to be! *Work, work, work* – that's all you ever think about.'

She fell into a sullen silence.

And John was also silent all the way to her front door, even then only saying 'See you around,' before Susannah slammed it in his face.

There was absolutely nothing else to say – except to himself. *'What a bloody fool I've been.'*

IIIIII

John knew that he shouldn't have a nightcap, not after that champagne at the Ritz – a drink he rarely touched because it usually went straight to his head. He had only ordered it on Susannah's insistence, but thank God had managed to restrict himself to one glass.

He was cross with himself, and even more with her, and depressed seeing Alice, realizing – if he were honest – that there hadn't been any girls as interesting as her since they split up. And try as he might to concentrate on tomorrow's presentation, it didn't work – to the point he almost felt like phoning her – that's if she had the same number of three years ago. No, that was crazy, he told himself. And she'd probably be in bed with her escort anyway.

What had he been doing for the last three years? Working long hours, certainly. The business was fine, in fact growing fast, but his personal life was once again a shambles. It had truly shaken him seeing Alice that evening, though he had sometimes imagined that moment, thinking it would be little more than 'a blast from the past' that he could dismiss quite easily. But it hadn't been like that at all.

In fact, it had bought the last three years into fast focus and all the mistakes he had made with women since breaking up with her. First with Joanna, a fitness trainer, fun to be with, but constantly complaining about the British weather and desperate to get back to Australia, her home country – which she eventually did, furious that he wouldn't go with her.

Then with Priya, an Indian girl whose parents strongly disapproved of her going out with a white man – that relationship was doomed from the start, with an ironic twist in reverse racism. After that, Amelia, an advertising copywriter who'd lost her job at J. Walter Thompson and couldn't find another one, eventually begging John to take her on which he refused to do, knowing it wouldn't work having her in the office all day. Followed by Anna, a fashion buyer, whose obsession with her wardrobe soon drove him mad. He had never seen a woman's bedroom with so many clothes, or one who agonized so endlessly about what to wear – and even what handbag to pick from the dozens she owned.

Who next? Maria, a trainee lawyer who worked such long hours he barely saw her, let alone in his bed. She was always too tired for any of that. And there were other women who had axed *him*, realizing that he was not in love with them, or not enough to make a go of it, mostly actresses and production assistants on the agency's commercials. Not only unwise choices, but also unprofessional.

He thought of Alice, wondering whether it would be possible to start again and whether the man she was with was a serious fixture. Perhaps Liz might know. He resolved to phone her after the presentation – and downing the last drop of Scotch, told himself to go to bed.

CHAPTER 8

PUTNEY, LONDON

Alice's old friend Jimmy Mason was staying at her house the following night, and she was glad of his company – especially as she'd heard nothing from Jean-Michel and didn't expect to. She and Jimmy had been friends for ages, but never more than that, and it was a relief to be able to tell him anything. Now, after a companionable evening and a takeaway curry, they were watching a riveting programme about the parlous state of Britain's prisons – a subject all over the news – when to her irritation the phone rang. She immediately felt guilty; after all, it might be one of Robin's sons calling.

'Hello.'

'Hi, Alice. It's me, John.'

The first time she'd heard his voice in three years, except when he was asking to change tables at The Ritz.

'Look, I'm really sorry about last night. I didn't know what to do. But I just couldn't sit next to you all evening, and I ….'

Alice interrupted him, 'Forget it. It doesn't matter.'

'It does to me. Seeing you brought everything flooding back. In fact, they've never really gone, and I …'

Alice cut in again, 'Well, I didn't exactly want to sit next to *you* either. Anyway ...'

This time it was John's turn to interrupt.

'Alice, *please* listen. The fact is, I've been missing you, and lately more and more. I'm surprised Liz hasn't told you.'

Alice didn't tell him that she had.

'Look,' she said, 'you can't simply dump someone and go back to the past just like that. It wouldn't work. At the very least, you need a breathing space.'

'I've had a breathing space for three years.'

Alice almost laughed. 'Hardly! Not from what Liz tells me. She says you've had a string of girlfriends ever since we split up.'

'That's the point, Alice. Doesn't that tell you something? None of them were right. And neither was the girl you saw. That's well and truly over. In fact, our dinner was a disaster.'

'Ditto ours,' retorted Alice.

She immediately regretted saying that. It might give John false hope.

There was an awkward silence before he continued: 'Look, can't we just meet up somewhere and have a chat?'

'I'm not sure it's a good idea. There's too much baggage between us.'

'Not for me. Not any more. I've got rid of it.'

Alice paused, remembering the past – both how good it had been and then finally how bad. At the end, all John had thought about was himself – with not a care in the world for her battered reputation, and moreover, her battered body when David Hammond had nearly killed her.

'Alice…you still there?'

'Yup.' She knew she sounded brisk. 'John, for goodness sake, you can't just jump from one person to another. That's an insult to the next one, and the previous one, come to that. And you don't take someone to The Ritz if you don't care about them.'

'I did care. But not enough. And certainly not now.'

There was a protracted pause before he continued.

'What if we leave it a couple of months? Could I call you then?'

'You could. But I'm not sure it's a good idea. You'd only rake things over.'

'Not any more. I've put the rake away.'

Alice sighed. 'Look, I'm sorry John, but I have to go. I've got someone here.'

John immediately pictured her handsome escort at The Ritz, and with a flash of envy.

'Okay, I'll call you in a month or so. And Alice, try not to find anyone else before then.' He knew he was probably saying that too late.

Alice was suddenly irritated. Why *shouldn't* she find someone else? He was talking as if he owned her.

'Bye then.' She hung up, now unable to concentrate on the programme – which irritated her even more.

Jimmy knew John quite well from the time when Alice was involved with him, and she decided to ask him for advice. He was also trained in psychology – in fact they had trained together – and he would be a good confidant.

But then, she knew only too well from her own ghastly mistakes that even psychologists could get things terribly wrong.

CHAPTER 9

NEW SCOTLAND YARD

'Tim, I'm really sorry to hear about your father.'

Alice and Tim Marshal had come to the Scotland Yard office of Joe Bain, now a Detective Inspector – the very same one where Robin Marshal used to work – with a fine view over the rooftops of Westminster. Joe had been Robin's right-hand man for years, and had also known his two sons from childhood, taking a real interest in what they were up to. Worryingly, he also knew that the elder one, Tim, now a recently qualified Detective Sergeant, would not have asked for this meeting unless it were something serious. And nor would Alice. She, too, went a long way back with him, not least during the traumas of the Hammond serial murder events three years ago.

He had begun by offering everyone coffee, once again irritated that this was the expected ritual even when there were clearly important things to discuss. Normally calm and amenable, he felt a familiar rush of irritation at the waste of time. But at last the meeting started.

'It's about Dad we came. And thanks for seeing us so quickly,' said Tim. 'Let me bring you up to speed. As you know, he retired early so he could look after Mum. Her Parkinson's isn't getting any easier – and can't get easier – and she's pretty well confined to a wheelchair now.'

Bain nodded. 'Yes, I heard. I was very sorry to hear that.'

'Thanks. Anyway, it all started so well, or at least as well as could be expected. Dad even took up gardening, and got an old police dog as a pet and it was all working out. Then two weeks ago, Mum was in her wheelchair in the house, and getting really worried that Dad hadn't appeared for some time. He never leaves her on her own that long. Suddenly the dog appeared, covered in blood. So she drove herself out into the garden and found Robin in a pool of blood in the garage. The ambulance came quickly enough, and Dad's now on the way to recovery, thank God.'

Tim was about to go on, but Joe put up his hand, shocked.

'Why didn't you tell me about this before? I heard about it when I got back from leave abroad on Monday, but not the details. Just something about an attempted burglary, not that Robin was injured. If I'd known, I'd have been in touch immediately and gone to visit. God, you must have thought I was very unfeeling after all these years.'

'No, not at all. And Dad wanted it hushed up, didn't want it made public and everyone knowing about it. He's become really secretive.'

Joe nodded, understanding why only too well. Retribution had become a threat for both police and prison service people. He took a deep breath. 'Okay, go on.'

'From what we can gather from Mum, Dad seemed to be expecting a stranger – a friend of a friend – to come and help him clear the garage. All clogged up with their things from London. Anyway, a man turned up and when they went to the garage, the guy pulled a knife and stabbed him. Dad fought back and the Alsatian went for the chap, who must have panicked and run off.'

'Good God, I had no idea,' said Bain, again visibly shocked. ' I never saw anything about it in the papers. Please give your father my very best wishes. And where's he now?'

'Still in hospital. Winchester Hospital.'

'Under guard, I hope.'

Tim nodded, to Bain's relief.

'I'll call them. Any idea who might have done it?'

'None. But Dad has,' said Tim. 'Actually, that's why we're here to see you. The fact is, he was pretty worried about retiring so early. He's even changed his appearance, growing a beard – you'd hardly recognise him. He always thought that someone he'd put away might go for him. You know, seek revenge. That's another reason he got out of town, to the country.'

No-one spoke for a moment, until Alice intervened.

'So we wondered if we could look back and try and find out who might hate him enough to attack him – or send someone else to do that, or even kill him. And we figure you might be the only person who could tell us, the only one who might know.'

'Hang on,' said Joe. 'You're making assumptions. It could have been just what I thought when I heard about it. A petty criminal, raiding the garage – or a local burglar. Although I *do* admit an armed one is rare.'

'We thought that, to start with,' said Tim. 'But the wounded dog was taken away too, and during surgery the vets found DNA in its jaw – human blood and hair. They usually test dogs to confirm if they've bitten people – you know, in civil damages or criminal negligence cases. But in this case, they were trying to find out *who* Benny had bitten. And my friends in the Hampshire police came back to me yesterday. The DNA came from a known thug called Rory McKillop. String of convictions, usually violent, GBH and ABH. In and out of jail. Released five months ago – from Belmarsh.

Significantly, he's a Scot, born in Stockport, who only ever operated in the North or the Midlands – Manchester, Leeds, Birmingham. So we have to ask ourselves what he was doing in a quiet village in leafy Hampshire, with a knife and stabbing a senior retired Met officer. Alice and I would like to know if he ever had anything to do with my father, or more likely, if someone who did might have put him up to it.'

There was a long silence, while Joe Bain stared at them. 'You know this is strictly against the rules.'

Now there was an even longer pause.

'But Robin and I do go back a long way,' added Bain. 'You have to promise me that you'll share anything I find with the proper authorities. And *not* do anything stupid.'

Alice and Tim nodded their assent, both chastened and worried that Joe didn't entirely believe them.

'Okay, assuming your theory, one of revenge, is perhaps right, let's look at what the computer tells us.'

They gathered round Joe's desk.

'First of all, it would surely have to be something pretty serious, someone with a really long jail sentence. Otherwise, it wouldn't be worth the candle to do anything like this.'

He began to click away at his keyboard.

'And, in my view, it would have to be fairly recent, with the anger still raw.'

Click. Click.

'There are six coming up. Let's have a look.' A long pause. 'Well, these two have died, so they're out. So that leaves four.

Then, to do something like that, let's assume they'd probably have a record of violence, or at least be used to it.' He tapped his pen on the screen. 'These two, Albert Jones and Elliot Francis, are in for fraud and computer crime. Crooks alright, but unlikely killers. Takes us down to two.'

Click.

'Seamus Morrissey? Can't be him, sent back two months ago to Ireland to face serious crimes there. That leaves…'

Click.

'Oh, shit! MacDonald.'

'Who's he?' asked Alice.

'I'd say one of the nastiest criminals around. James Dougal

MacDonald, who likes to call himself 'Big Mack'. There might be a possible link there. Robin nailed him for attempted murder in 2008, but he was sure that he had more on him than just attempted murder. In fact, he thought he'd personally killed several people, and probably organised the killing of several more.

He *really* is big, about six four, and pumped up with body-building. Shaven-headed, ugly and tattooed. And probably gay, or bisexual. And the trouble is he's as intelligent as he's evil.' Joe leaned forward and looked at the screen. 'That's *really* interesting. He's currently in for nine more years and in Belmarsh. Same jail as McKillop was in. You can't draw conclusions from that, but...'

He turned to them and sipped his coffee.

'In the old days, as we used to say, being sent to prison meant that you could do no more harm. Politicians were always mouthing off about how society was now protected.' He laughed, but bitterly.

'Not any more. First of all, the prisons are in a mess. There are now about twice the prisoners compared with, say, in Thatcher's time. Over eighty thousand. And with less, not more, prison officers to look after them. The prisoners have a miserable time, locked in their cells for far too long – eighteen hours a day or more. So there's terrific tension and danger for everyone. Small wonder prison officers are leaving in droves, including pals of mine. It's underpaid and it's now increasingly physically dangerous. In some of the privately-run prisons there's just *one* pair of handcuffs and you have to apply for *permission* to use them. Not very helpful when facing a riot.

And prisoner morale is at rock-bottom too. Not much training, little rehabilitation. That's why so many of them are committing suicide.

And then there are the drugs. I've never quite understood it, but prisons are stuffed with them. Inmates can go in clean and come out addicts. And there's big money to be made from drugs, especially in prison.

So I think you'll find that 'Big Mack' could be living the life of a right Robber Baron. He'd have his own people on the inside and lots more on the outside. Using fear and money together. It's a truly ironic situation that to get *really* rich, a criminal has to go to jail. And if he wanted to go after someone like Robin, he probably wouldn't have that much difficulty. Robin was quite right to be anxious.'

'Do you think it could be him?'

'I've no idea,' Joe shrugged. '*And I repeat, neither do you*. And it's not for you to find out. I'll pass on what you've said, and what I've found, and then I'd suggest you keep well out of it. I don't need to tell you, assumptions are dangerous. Very dangerous. I owe a great deal to Robin, but the last thing he'd want is you getting yourself into trouble by getting involved, asking too many questions, and probably putting yourselves in danger – especially you, Alice.

I'll do what I can, but I must ask you to back off. There are any one of dozens of burglars who might have done this.'

'But *armed* ones?' asked Alice.

'Yes, even armed ones. Guns are traceable, knives are not. Anyone can get a knife.'

'But don't you see our point, Joe, that it could be due to revenge?'

'Of course. But it's far too early to jump to conclusions. And if I may remind you again Alice, that's not your job. You've done fantastic work helping us in the past, especially with Hammond for instance, but there are times to back off. And this is one of them. Leave the police to do their job, and I'll do my best to make sure they do.'

||||||

LOCKED IN **FEAR**

Twenty minutes later, Alice was sitting with Tim in a bay window of a pub in Victoria round the corner from the Scotland Yard building, still horrified by what Joe Bain had told them about prisons in general – and people like 'Big Mack' in particular. And also slightly disappointed with Joe Bain's attitude.

'I hope Joe hasn't become a bit of an old woman since he's been promoted,' said Tim, sipping a beer. 'An awful lot of talk about rules.'

'I know what you mean. And I'm not at all sure I'm prepared to wait around for the police to get themselves in gear. Whoever it was might try to do in your Dad again. Do you think it's that Mack fellow?'

'I don't know. Probably. But I wouldn't know how to prove it.'

'But *I* might,' said Alice. 'And I've got an excuse to try.'

CHAPTER 10

PUTNEY

Alice had at last been persuaded to meet up with John again by her old friend Liz, but not in a twosome – instead accompanied by Liz and her husband Derek, and somewhere near her home so she could make an easy escape if things didn't work out.

Now she and Liz were sitting in a quiet corner of 'The Duke's Head' – a riverside pub a short stroll from Alice's house, ideal if at any point she felt uncomfortable and needed a quick exit. Dinner afterwards had been suggested by Liz at a nearby Kashmiri restaurant, but Alice had firmly decided to keep her options open on that, deciding it could all be too much too soon. After all, she hadn't seen John in three years.

What to wear? John had always liked her in violet colours which matched her unusual eyes, so she had also firmly decided against that, not wanting to give out any obvious signals, instead opting for a simple blue polo sweater and grey trousers, a classic understatement. Anything to keep things cool and low key in such difficult circumstances.

'Glass of wine while we're waiting?' asked Liz.

'Think I'd rather have a Bloody Mary', smiled Alice.

'Good idea. I could do with one, too.'

Alice suddenly realized that Liz was also tense, wondering how the evening would progress and whether this reunion would be impossibly fraught. And no doubt John would be feeling that too.

'Here, get that down you.' Liz returned from the bar with two glasses.

'Double shots, which reminds me of your shooting. I'm amazed you never told me about that before.'

'Guess I wanted to keep it secret in case I was useless at it. But incredibly, I took to it like a duck to water.'

Liz laughed. 'And is that what you shoot? Ducks?'

'No, just clays. Don't think I could cope with the live stuff. Anyway, I found I wasn't bad at it, and now I take part in competitions all over England. But the best ones are called the 'Coupe des Nations', the French against the English. We're called the Swallows, and the French girls the Amazons, and there's a friendly shoot-out weekend once a year. Good fun. It all started with men's clubs in London like Boodle's and Buck's when they got together with their equivalents in France. All men at first, but now it's women, too.

Every year, we alternate between France and Britain and go to really great places – even castles and chateaux. Costs a bomb, but luckily it's only once a year. Another world, really. All the French seem to be Barons or Counts with castles and chateaux of their own – as if their Revolution never happened. And last year – our turn to be hosts – we were at Castle Howard – a hundred and fifty rooms, with ten thousand acres, where they filmed 'Brideshead Revisited' I remarked to one of the Frenchmen how lovely it was, and you'll never believe what he said. 'Yes, larger than some of ours, but smaller and less elegant than others.' And he meant his *team's* castles, not France's!'

'Good Lord, Alice. I must say, you seem to move in exalted circles!'

'Hardly. It's only a once a year event, as I said. Couldn't afford more. And they're interesting rather than exalted. I've even met one elegant old chap who sold religious paintings in Paris who suddenly admitted quite calmly how he'd once tried to assassinate de Gaulle. Told me he planted a bomb under a garden path which de Gaulle was due to walk down, but that the gardener screwed things up by watering the flowers and shorting the wires to the explosive.'

Liz had no time to absorb this extraordinary story. Suddenly, John and Derek were with them.

Alice knew John well enough to know that he would have been relieved to see her talking so animatedly to Liz – not sitting there silently, ashen-faced. So far, so good she thought. But there was a big 'but'. Not easy to meet someone who was once the love of your life after a three year gap and keep things cool, especially after such an acrimonious split on his part.

But it turned out to be surprisingly easy.

'Right, what are we having?' asked John cheerily (or doing his best to sound cheery, thought Alice) as he surveyed their almost empty glasses.

'Well, it *was* Bloody Marys,' said Liz, 'but it's probably better to switch to wine. Get a bottle of something and we'll divvy up later.'

John disappeared off to the bar, smoothing his flyaway hair as he went. Alice smiled, remembering when they had first met how his crazy hair had reminded her of Boris Johnson. And to her surprise, she felt a sudden rush of affection, though quickly telling herself that the feeling was far too fast, too soon. Three years was a long time; and both of them needed to be cautious to see if things were reparable – or indeed, even manageable, however cheery the others managed to make this reunion.

'Would you believe,' said Liz to her husband, 'Alice is now a shooting champion? She's in a team that competes with France every year.'

'Hardly a champion!' laughed Alice. 'It's not a national team. And you don't have to be that good to compete. Just competent, like me. I only really go for the fun of it, hoping not to make a fool of myself. And even if I did, I don't think it would matter that much. It's all a friendly, and a nice way of meeting new people.'

She suddenly recalled that John had seen her in the Ritz with Jean-Michel, and spotting him returning from the bar, decided to change the subject.

'Anyway, how are you two?' she asked Derek and Liz.

'Pretty good, actually,' said Derek. 'Did Liz give you the good news?'

'No. What?'

'We only heard yesterday. We're having a baby. It's finally worked, the IVF. Third time lucky!'

'Oh, that's *marvellous*! Congratulations!'

John was suddenly back with a bottle of rosé and four glasses. Alice looked at the label, touched he recalled her favourite brand. She looked up at him, smiling.

'Thanks. You remembered.'

'Not much I haven't.'

That would go for the bad times as well as the good ones, she thought . But she forced another smile.

'Anyway, let's raise a glass to Liz and Derek and their new baby. That's wonderful news.'

She could see that John wanted to get the subject back to them, but she wasn't going there for now, especially in front of the others. Too fast, too soon, after all that time apart. Softly, softly, she told herself.

'So how's the job going?' asked John.

'Interesting, pretty good. Depressing at times as it always is, but I get enough breaks to think it's worthwhile.'

'A bit like advertising, then. One minute I wonder what the hell I'm doing, and the next I know. But I never know if I'm really *adding* anything, well anything worthwhile to help the human race. Not like your job. I have to say, I envy you that.'

Alice fell silent, remembering the good times with John. He had always been incredibly supportive of her professional life.

Half an hour later, Derek drank back the last of his wine. 'Anyway, who's coming to celebrate with us?'

'A bit early,' laughed Liz. 'We've got nine months to go!'

'I'm on,' said John, glancing at Alice.

'Me, too,' she replied, to his evident relief.

|||||||

Alice's landline rang the next evening.

She picked up the phone, fearing it might be one of Robin's sons with bad news, but it was John.

'Hi, it's me. Good to see you last night.'

'Nice to see you, too.'

'Look, I wondered if you were up to a dinner on our own, somewhere we can talk?'

Alice wavered. Seeing John again had been pleasant, far easier than she'd expected. But a vague rapprochement with other people around was one thing, a reunion alone quite another. And the bad memories still fought with the good ones, although considerably less these days.

'I'm not sure,' she answered.

'Let's give it a go, Alice. And if it doesn't work out – well, you can tell me to get lost. I know I deserve that now.'

Alice laughed. 'You don't. You didn't. You had good reasons for getting out.'

'Not good enough ones. I know that now.'

Neither spoke for a moment.

'Look, John, you can't just jump from one girl to another. That's insulting to both of them, as I told Liz. And you can't go back in time that easily either. Too much baggage. And to be honest, we've probably both changed. Three years is a heck of a long time. Maybe better to leave things as they are. Or *were*.'

'I can't. And I don't want to.'

Alice was flattered, but not persuaded.

'I'll think about it, and then I'll call you.'

'Please do that. But don't make it too long.'

CHAPTER 11

BIGHTON, HAMPSHIRE

'I said I had a plan.' Alice was sitting opposite Robin Marshal and his son Tim. Pam was away in Winchester – with her carer, for a physiotherapy session.

'I talked to Joe Bain about all this and he mentioned that he'd served years ago with the Deputy Governor of Belmarsh, called Mary Bloomfield. She and Joe had been at the Police College at Bramshill and become quite friendly. Apparently, after a while she then transferred to the prison service.

So I asked Joe to get in touch with her, and as a favour, see if he could get me into Belmarsh as a psychologist for two months during the summer holiday period. I told him to use the very real excuse that I have two patients who are prisoners' wives and that I wanted to understand more about their problems.

Anyway, Mary said yes.'

'What?' Robin blurted out, startled. 'That could be *really* dangerous.'

'Well, what could be more dangerous than you being knifed in your own garage?' retorted Alice, maybe a bit too breezily 'And anyway, I'll be a member of staff, not a prisoner. I won't be in any danger.'

'From what I've heard, life's bloody dangerous for staff as well these days. And why do it? Do you really need to?' It was Tim's turn to be anxious.

'We need to know more. We *suspect* this Big Mack fellow, but we can't be sure. And unless we really know who it is, we can't stop him. I'm certain I can find out more from other inmates. Trust me, I have absolutely no intention of meeting Big Mack himself. They probably wouldn't let me anyway.'

'No,' said Robin, 'maybe not, but I bet you won't be able to resist digging around among people who might know something. That's stupid, Alice. And if I may remind you, you've taken ages to recover from all this kind of thing before. Consorting with, well, what most would call thoroughly unsavoury people. You're a psychiatrist, Alice, *not* a detective. Keep out of it, and let the police do what they're trained to – and what you're not.'

He sighed deeply.

'When will you *ever* learn to keep out of deep water? Fond as I am of you, I sometimes think you're a complete fool. And now is one of those times. Probing prisoners is not, I repeat *not* your job. And even if you come to conclusions, they won't be valid, just conjecture.'

'I did okay with that woman who chucked her husband down the stairs', said Alice defiantly.

'I know,' said Robin, 'but that was different, very different. She was hardly a known killer. Not a female 'Big Mack', with a string of convictions. And anyway, nobody's going to squeak about Big Mack, and certainly not to you. They've got their own skins to worry about."

This retort was followed by nearly half an hour of really quite heated argument, as both father and son tried to dissuade her from what they obviously thought was a ridiculously hazardous and unnecessary venture.

Alice was therefore quite relieved to hear a car as Pam and her carer suddenly returned. And when they came in, Alice leaned over the wheelchair and kissed Pam, pretending that she'd just dropped in long enough to see how Robin was getting along with his recovery – and then slipped quickly away after a polite interval.

She was determined to carry out her reconnaissance plan – in spite of her friends' very understandable misgivings.

||||||

However, Alice soon seriously wondered herself if she was doing the right thing volunteering for prison work at Belmarsh. Yes, a greater knowledge of prison existence would almost certainly help her to advise her two patients whose husbands were doing time. But she knew her real motive was to find out more about Big Mack and whether he could possibly be the mastermind behind the attack on Robin. But, as Robin and his sons had both said so forcibly, that was a job for the police, not for a psychologist. And deep down she knew that they were right.

Even so, she decided to go ahead, telling herself – or probably fooling herself – she owed it to her patients. How could you really tell what life was like in prisons without seeing inside them and listening to prisoners themselves, even though you had access to prison reports as she sometimes did? And how could you support prisoners' wives for an extended period – maybe five or ten years or even longer – without really seeing what they saw, feeling what they felt first-hand? And it wasn't just wives who were suffering, of course. It was their children too – all under sentence themselves, condemned to endless queues on visiting days, their mouths and hair searched for drugs, each one of them being suspected of being a drug mule, however young.

She also remembered all too vividly from childhood how tedious and boring long journeys could be – with that endless question 'Are we nearly there?' And trains would be even worse with endless delays due to weekend repairs. And it would be more distressing still for kids having to visit their Dads at weekends – missing time with their friends, and of course, those all-important birthday parties.

She knew only too well that prison wives were split into two categories – those who were frankly relieved to be shot of their husbands – despite any lost earnings – and those who weren't – finding each day a struggle, especially if they had children – and particularly on visiting days that were always harrowing and demeaning and too far apart and too short to maintain any meaningful contact. At least her two patients were literate, able to text and write letters as many weren't.

And her two patients still loved their husbands – that was clear. Enough to put up with being herded almost like cattle in the outside yards until ten a.m., strongly discouraged to talk to other visitors, coping with children who were probably frightened of the place, and maybe hardly remembered what their fathers were like, let alone why they'd been banged up – indeed, if they'd ever been told.

She'd heard it all, or enough to sympathize about the trauma of visiting days – plastic chairs for the visitors bolted to the floors, the depressing and distressing noise of a visiting area – with no soft furnishings to dumb it down, and the sheer hopelessness on returning home that could make nights sleepless and day-to-day life a constant struggle. It was a blessing for the prisoners' wives she treated that they could afford psychiatric help at all, thanks to friends and relatives and help from the NHS. How many others were suffering in silence? Thousands, probably.

If she didn't owe it to Robin and his sons to find out more about Big Mack, she felt she owed it to her patients to see prison life first-hand. And maybe, she thought, just maybe, she could kill two birds with one stone.

But would anyone squeak? Unlikely. As Robin had reminded her, they had themselves to think about, not her – a middle-class female psychologist about as removed from them as anyone they could imagine, and with people inside with them like 'Big Mack' who'd be the first to know if anyone spilt the beans about other inmates. And no doubt take revenge, in the highly unlikely event they did.

CHAPTER 12

PUTNEY

At seven-thirty in the evening, Alice opened her front door to see John with a beautiful bunch of tulips, relieved that it wasn't the red roses that he used to buy her. On their first date out together after three years, that would have been far too much of a statement.

'Thanks John, they're lovely!'

She took the bouquet and they exchanged kisses on both cheeks.

'Go into the sitting-room while I fetch a vase, and help yourself to the jug of Bloody Mary. She pointed. 'It's over there. I'll be back in a minute.'

John poured himself a drink and looked around him. The room was exactly as he remembered, full of books and comfortable old furniture. Absolutely the opposite of Susannah's almost bookless flat – pretty well the norm nowadays, he thought ruefully. Just the other day he'd read in the papers that only twenty per cent of people's homes had a single book in them. Depressing.

But sitting on the sofa and placing his glass on a side-table, he noticed one difference – a large, silver-framed photo of what looked like a shooting party. A group of men and a few women with their guns in sleeves was standing in front of an imposing and beautiful chateau. And there in the front row was Alice – next to the very same man he'd seen with her at The Ritz. He looked at him more closely. Were they an item, or just friends? If they were just friends, The Ritz would have surely been a bit over the top. And if they were an item, would Alice have agreed to this date?

Suddenly Alice was there with the vase, noticing him replace the frame.

'That was a shooting party I went on recently, in France.'

'Gosh, I didn't know you shot!'

'I didn't 'til recently. But only clay pigeons. I took it up about a year ago.'

'Good Lord.' He glanced at the photo again. 'They look like a fun bunch of people.'

'They are. That's half the reason I go. More than half, probably. It's a real break from depressed patients. A complete change of scene.'

Alice guessed that he might have spotted her escort at The Ritz in the photo, but thankfully he chose to change the subject. Anyway, Jean-Michel hadn't called her since then. That relationship was over before it had scarcely begun.

'So, where would you like to go for dinner?' He had assumed, rightly, that they wouldn't be eating in, not on the first date together after so long. Too intimate, too soon.

'Well, if you don't mind, I've booked 'Bill's' – a new place in the High Street. Well, not that new, it's been there about two years. Good brasserie food and nice buzzy atmosphere.'

John was relieved. A lively brasserie might help if things got awkward. Noise to fill in any awkward silences.

'Fine by me.'

Alice looked at her watch. 'I've booked for eight. So we've got a bit of time. We don't need to go for a quarter of an hour. That's if we go by car.'

'Fine. I'll take mine.'

The next fifteen minutes were slightly strained for both of them, neither of them wanting to pry into the other's life – or at least the romantic side of it, and wondering if things could ever return to where they were, and Alice absolutely knew that she must avoid any mention of Robin and her plans to visit Belmarsh – a sure-fire way to put him off.

She had purposely booked a table close to the door in case she needed a speedy exit. But as the evening progressed, and in the convivial surroundings, both of them relaxed a bit. It was an auspicious new start, although Alice couldn't help remembering what her godmother Aunt Helen had always told her about the wartime years with couples getting reunited after long absences – and how difficult, indeed impossible, it often was.

'How are your parents?' she had asked, after a while.

'Dad's not too good – a bit of heart trouble, but thankfully not too serious, and Mum's okay. Anyway, I've told her I wanted to see you again.'

Alice was surprised. 'And how did she take it?'

John paused.

'Not too well, too be honest. We'll cross that bridge when we come to it.'

A pretty silly expression, thought Alice. 'There may not be a bridge when you come to it. Or it might be blocked by a couple of Panzer divisions.'

He grinned, suddenly remembering that Alice loved war films, and especially 'A Bridge Too Far' about the failure at Arnhem. How many other girls he knew enjoyed war films? He couldn't think of any. Nor, for that matter, any who'd taken up shooting or were psychologists competent enough to work with the police. So different from the pretty, but mostly empty-headed girls he'd been dating for so long.

'And how's your Dad, Alice?

'Fine. I'm taking a few days off in France to see him soon.'

'And doing some clay shooting, I expect?'

'No, the French competition is always in May – so that's not for another year now.'

'Nice to have a new hobby like that. In fact, I've gone back to one I had as a kid – building and flying model planes. Mind you, it's all far more advanced than it used to be, with really clever radio control. I'm a member of what's called the LMA, the Large Model Association, and we go to air shows all over the place. If you like, you can come with me to Richmond Park where some of us meet to practise.'

Alice pictured it, imagining sophisticated model planes and their eccentric owners. 'Actually, I wouldn't mind that. It sounds rather fun.'

First time any girl has said that to me, thought John, pleased by her interest.

When he drove her home in the old Morgan she remembered so well, she didn't offer him a night-cap as he guessed she wouldn't. But at least there was a light kiss on the lips before she got out of the car, thanking him for dinner.

'Want to do this again?' he asked tentatively.

Alice paused. 'Yes, I think I do.'

'So it's au revoir?'

'Oui,' she smiled.

Alice didn't go to bed straight away, tired as she was, instead deciding to have a last glass of wine and think things over. They had certainly gone far better than she had anticipated.

After a while she decided to check her computer to see if there were any messages.

There was one.

Dear Alice,

Wondered if you'd like to meet up again. Was a bit worried about you in The Ritz – probably something on your mind, and I didn't want to pry.

Anyway, I'll be in London in two weeks and would really like to see you again.

Or if you can't do that, why not come to France later?
A bientôt.
Jean-Michel x

Alice stared at the message, suddenly in a total quandary, her mind caught up in a whirlwind of conflicting thoughts. Would the past always be hovering between her and John, however much either of them fooled themselves it wouldn't?

And if Jean-Michel wanted to give things another go, might it be better to make a completely fresh start with someone else, and probably in a different country? But how happy would she be to live somewhere she couldn't work, at least as a psychologist, neither having a good enough grasp of French nor the relevant requirements to work there under different medical rules? She reminded herself she was really jumping the gun. After all, they'd only had one date, and a pretty disastrous one at that.

Moreover, she knew she could never be a 'chatelaine', looking after some vast country pile, like almost all the wives of the French 'Coupe des Nations' team. Nor would she enjoy spending most of the rest of her time raiding boutiques, as the French women did.. While the men went shooting, the women always went shopping – not Alice's bag at all – even if she had the money to do so. She had enough, but certainly not *that* much.

And what they bought – on the one occasion she had accompanied them – amazed her. One of them had been in the process of buying an exquisite chandelier when she dropped it on to the stone floor of the boutique, smashing it to smithereens. Alice had watched agog as she simply took her wallet out of her Hermes bag and fished out a huge wad of what must have been thousands of euros with scarcely a blink.

Against all that, if it worked out with John this time, it probably never would with his parents, and that might drive a wedge between them. It was clear they were very close, and, of course, he was an only son. And she was still scarred by the totally unfeeling way he had dumped her in Starbucks, almost next to where they had just eaten. The memory of that had come flooding back to her as they passed the café, as it almost certainly had to him – or why had he suddenly tightened his grip on her arm on the way to his car, as if to reassure her?

And if she were in this sort of quandary, would it be better to see neither of them? Although none of her boyfriends over the last three years had been nearly as attractive and interesting as either John *or* Jean-Michel.

Her mobile suddenly rang.

'Just thought I'd say goodnight. It was really good to see you.'

It was John.

Suddenly she knew what to do. Somebody down the road, not eight hundred miles away. Someone who clearly hadn't forgotten her as she hadn't him, despite their acrimonious parting. Maybe, just maybe, it was worth another try.

CHAPTER 13

BELMARSH PRISON, WOOLWICH

Before committing herself to work at Belmarsh – assuming she would be accepted – Alice decided to work out the logistics of getting there, by car or public transport. She already knew it wouldn't be easy – the place was about as far away as possible to choose in London.

She first checked out public transport, but sitting in front of her computer, the results were depressing. First, she'd have to walk to Barnes Station – at least twenty minutes. Then go by overland rail to Waterloo – another twenty-three minutes. After that, she'd have to go back *across* the river to Cannon Street, perhaps half an hour. Then take the train to Woolwich Arsenal, another twenty-five minutes. And she *still* wouldn't be there. She'd then have to wait for a number 240 bus for the prison. Probably another twenty minutes. The whole thing would take an age.

Four hours of the day gone, just on travelling – and even that was assuming no rail strikes, delays or disruptions – unless she rented somewhere nearby.

She was almost thinking of giving up. All that travelling and slogging to and fro with a heavy bag and a laptop, and in an unusually hot August – and in trains and buses not properly air-conditioned. And on top of all that was the inconvenience of re-arranging her patient schedules unless she took time at Belmarsh during her holidays.

But she felt she owed it to Robin and his wife to make the effort.

She decided it might be better to try to drive there, getting up really early in the morning. And before that, a reconnaissance would be necessary – on a quiet Sunday, but knowing it would take far longer with the traffic on a working day.

After leaving her house, she crossed the Thames over Putney Bridge and set off down the King's Road, turning on to the elegant Chelsea Embankment, all still familiar to her. But things soon began to change. Thank goodness, she thought, she had a satnav to guide her through the maze of south-east London.

Its voice now told her to turn right before the Houses of Parliament, cross the river over Lambeth Bridge, and then turn east past Lambeth Palace towards Waterloo Station.

And now it all began to become very unfamiliar.

She was startled by the amount of new buildings springing up everywhere – hugely ambitious and tall structures, which wouldn't even have been envisaged only a few years before. And with funny names like the 'Gherkin' and the 'Shard'. The contrast of small shops and neatly-terraced houses with these mammoth megaliths amazed her – as if monsters and minnows were somehow living together. But how happily, she wondered? This thought continued for the rest of her journey. It was also strange to see small and beautiful old churches in the lee of vast financial headquarters, as if God and Mammon were living side by side.

Having always – and mostly secretly – been afraid of heights, she wondered if she could ever have worked in one of those vast structures, picturing what had been knocked down to make room for them all. Change everywhere. But a change for the better?

'Blast!' she suddenly blurted out. Because, thinking about change, they'd blocked Tooley Street and the satnav hadn't known. She was forced to cross over London Bridge, do an illegal U-turn , come back across and set off all over again.

After half an hour in totally unfamiliar territory, she passed the magnificent palace at Greenwich. At least nobody had touched *that*, she thought with relief.

At last she was in the Belmarsh Prison car park, and facing a thick concrete wall about twenty feet high which almost entirely obscured the buildings behind it, and with a rounded bulbous top obviously intended to be impossible to scale.

Alice looked at her watch. The journey had taken her almost an hour and a quarter. It would be twice that, or even more, in the traffic on a weekday.

She would have to get up at five in the morning!

||||||

Now it was for real. Alice had been emailed with instructions to go to the staff car park, and after reporting to the gate, was quickly escorted to the office of the Deputy Governor, who shook her hand warmly.

'Hello, Alice. Thanks for coming. I'm Mary, Mary Bloomfield.'

Alice was slightly surprised to be greeted by a smartly-dressed, rather pretty and engaging tall blonde woman, probably only a couple of years older than herself.

What had she imagined? Someone much tougher-looking, and just because she worked in a prison? She reminded herself of the danger of pre-conceived notions.

'Hi. Good of you to see me.'

Mary offered Alice a seat in her quite spacious office and suggested coffee.

'Thanks. Black please, no sugar.'

Returning with two mugs, Mary surveyed Alice for a moment. It was not often that psychologists volunteered their services as she had, and particularly not one who had been personally involved with a now notorious killer – David Hammond – three years ago, albeit for only three dates. What did that say about Alice's judgement she had wondered, ever since her application to work at Belmarsh, and how many of the inmates would recognise her?

However, she quickly reminded herself of Alice's calm and impressive performance recently in the well-publicised trial of Ruth Lerner who had been acquitted of the murder of her husband.

'Joe Bain,' Mary said, 'who I served with when I was with the police years ago, told me you wanted to broaden your understanding of prison life.'

'Yes.'

'And mainly because you have patients who are prisoners' wives.'

Alice nodded. 'Yes.'

'And that you're willing to do a fill-in stint in the summer when we're short-staffed due to the holidays.'

'That's right.'

'Well, I think it would be helpful if I briefed you a bit about Belmarsh.'

'Yes, thanks.'

Mary took a deep breath. 'Well, it's a curious place, a mixture. It's best known, of course, as a Category A prison for really dangerous men, terrorists and so on, plus lots of notorious criminals like Ronnie Biggs, the train robber. But we've had many other prominent people here who aren't really villains in that sense – politicians like Jonathan Aitken and Jeffrey Archer, and Andy Coulson – David Cameron's press secretary – oh, and fraudsters like Azil Nadir.

It's also a local prison serving South East London and Essex, and Woolwich Crown Court, and with a Youth Offender section. So, a pretty busy place.

There are various blocks holding different categories of prisoner.

You wouldn't need to go into these because the prisoners, your patients, would be brought to you under escort, and of course with a full briefing on their backgrounds in advance.

Who's in here? There's a slight majority of black prisoners, about sixty per cent, with the rest white and some Muslims. Some of the terrorists *are* genuine Muslims, but the number tends to swell near Ramadan because the word's got out that the food for Muslims is much better in the evenings. Then there's a positive rush to be Muslim!' She smiled wryly, shaking her head.

'I won't pretend this is a very happy place. We suffer like all other prisons from too many inmates and too few, and underpaid, staff. That means prisoners are locked up, or 'banged up' as they say, for far too long – sometimes eighteen hours or more. That's really bad for morale. And there have been lots of complaints – even in Parliament, as I'm sure you know.

Depression, as I'm sure you also know, is a major problem in prisons. I'd estimate that up to two thirds of the prisoners here are depressed at any one time, with a number of acute sufferers. And our staff can also become depressed and demoralised – for instance our dedicated searchers, those who check the visitors, all with high responsibility but low pay.

Then, of course, there are the insidious pressures which wear prisoners down. Smaller ones, certainly, but still a constant drain on morale. Perpetual noise, with no soft furnishings to deaden the sound. Iron-barred gates endlessly being slammed, or locked and unlocked. And the constant smell of disinfectant even, and the lack of any home comforts – no curtains at cell windows, for example. But as I said earlier, it's the time prisoners spend stuck in their cells that *really* wears them down – one reason why our religious services are surprisingly well-attended. Often not much to do with God and Allah, I'm afraid. Anything to get out of their cells for an hour or two.

Our primary aim is, of course, protecting the public, but protecting our inmates and staff is also an uphill battle. In fact, all our staff have to undergo rigorous training in restraining attack or self-harm. If you came to work here, you'd probably be treating people who may have attempted suicide – although, amazingly, more kill themselves *after* release. They can't get jobs easily, have problems with relationships, and some even miss the comradeship and routine of life inside.'

Mary paused for a sip of coffee.

'One bit of support we *do* get with potential suicides are the 'listeners', of course.'

'Listeners?'

'Yes, inmates prepared to talk to any prisoners who seem vulnerable or depressed. Very respected and they get certain privileges. All thoroughly vetted and checked out, of course. Or as far as we can do that.

Prisoner safety is a constant problem, compounded by sexual frustration. Our eighteen to twenty-one year old inmates never share a cell with someone older. And our fifteen to eighteen year olds are housed in a different building. On top of all that, we've got the constant problem of accommodating very different religions. Everything from C of E and Sikh to Rastafarian.'

She poured them both more coffee.

'I'm sure I don't have to tell you about the critical new factor in all of this – drugs.' She sighed deeply.

'God, where to start? First, over half the prisoners here are in because of drugs, mostly stealing to pay for them. Then about the same proportion inside are still on them, and serious ones, especially crack cocaine and heroin. And it's getting worse. A few years ago, it was about ten per cent on heroin here. Now it's probably thirty. And one reason is the law, which has a built-in flaw. If an inmate is found taking any drugs in prison, including cannabis, he gets a month added to his sentence. But heroin can be flushed out of the body in twenty-four hours, so it's the one drug that's not easily detected. So addicts, idiotically, switch from comparatively harmless stuff like cannabis to really dangerous and addictive heroin and then become hooked.'

Alice knew enough about prison life not to start protesting naively about how on earth this could happen in places that were meant to be secure. Instead, she confined herself to questions of professional interest, some of which she was familiar with in her private practice.

'I suppose the so-called 'legal highs' are a problem as well?'

Mary nodded. 'You're right. The cannabinoids. And they've contributed to a huge increase of assaults on prison staff – especially the stimulants and the psychedelics. We don't much mind the 'downers', they just make the inmates sleepy and a bit forgetful. And, if I'm honest, easier to cope with. But, of course, all these drugs are far more dangerous when mixed with other things – then the outcome is completely unpredictable.

And on top of all that there's the Human Rights Act. It sometimes means that staff think they can't really search visitors properly, at least not as thoroughly as they've been trained to. So the stuff comes pouring in, usually via partners – in women's hair, ears, mouths – transferred during kissing or embracing, or even when fondling babies – with the drugs hidden in their nappies, of course. And it's not just wives and girlfriends bringing in the stuff. Incredibly, it's even priests and lawyers, too, no doubt bribed by payments outside.

And I won't pretend that our staff are all immune – a few 'joeys' or grams of heroin can double their meagre salaries, after all. They don't even have to be corrupt – just ineffective. The staff who search the visitors are the most junior and the most poorly-paid. We've seen them being browbeaten by aggressive and manipulative visitors.

Visitors often think *they're* the victims, really anti-establishment and anti-prison. Unless they've been given cast-iron intelligence on stuff coming in, staff aren't going to take a baby from its mother and remove its clothing, nappy and all.

Prisoners sometimes even swallow a condom full of heroin just before they're sent here and then retrieve it from their cell loo later. Very dangerous if they burst inside them – that means certain death.

And small quantities can get in hidden in legal documents, under postage stamps or the flaps of envelopes or even in Sikh turbans and inside the studs of football boots. You'd be amazed how resourceful smugglers can be.

And now the pushers are using drones to deliver, as you probably know. The ingenuity and effort's all extraordinary, but from *their* point of view it's worth it. After all, they fetch ten times or more here what it's worth on the street. Believe it or not, some cons are re-offending just to get back into jail to get dealing again – and earning hundreds of thousands of pounds a year.'

Alice found it hard to believe what she was hearing. 'But how can prisoners possibly afford it?'

'They can't, but their contacts on the outside can.'

'Good Lord.' Alice couldn't contain her astonishment. In spite of the fact that she knew something about all this, the details were still a revelation. She decided to broach the subject that most interested her, while not appearing too inquisitive.

'I suppose there are some prisoners who become bosses of these drugs enterprises?'

'Certainly, and they're much more powerful and ruthless than in the past – because the stakes are so much higher. These days we'd consider an old-timer like Frankie Fraser to be almost a gentleman. Now they stop at nothing to make sure they can keep going.

We've got several like that here in Belmarsh, and most of them are clever. They make themselves inconspicuous and their influence is insidious, subtle.'

Alice decided not to follow this line of questioning too far, lest it make Mary suspicious of her real motives. She wondered how long it would take to find out enough about 'Big Mack' – if she could at all.

After another few minutes, Mary suggested that Alice came with her to meet the medical staff and see her future consulting room – that's if her application were approved and if Alice were still committed.

Mary doubted she would be. A comfortable room in Putney in which to see her patients was a world away from Belmarsh. And why would a woman who'd been involved in a sensational murder trial like the Hammond one want to be involved with more criminals, even if it were to help her patients whose partners were serving time?

She decided to think about Alice's application for a few days before coming to any decision. Although liking her, the strict vetting process might prove to be a problem.

Someone on the Board of Governors might strongly object to a counsellor who had been personally linked with a serial killer of such notoriety, and understandably.

Mary accompanied Alice to the entrance where they shook hands warmly.

'By the way, Alice, congratulations on the Ruth Isaacs case. At least, OCD isn't a big problem here. At least, not yet.' She laughed. 'Frankly it's about the only problem we don't have.

Anyway I'll get your application processed as soon as I can and come back to you. I hope you don't mind me mentioning this, but the one thing that worries me is your involvement in the Hammond case.'

'I knew that might come up.'

'It might prove to be a hurdle,' replied Mary, 'but let's cross fingers.'

Four days later, Mary was able to phone Alice to tell her that her application had been accepted by a six to four vote majority after a first split vote.

Pleased and relieved, but also highly apprehensive, Alice couldn't help wondering if she were doing the right thing, especially as she would have to keep it quiet from Robin and Tim Marshal. What did she *really* know about prison life, apart from what Mary had told her, and what she'd gleaned from the media and a few patients with partners inside?

Would she suddenly be right out of her depth? And on top of that, would male prisoners really open up to a woman, and a middle-class one at that, with a voice and demeanour that was probably utterly alien? It was only some comfort that Mary Bloomfield had accepted her.

Too late, she rather wished she hadn't.

CHAPTER 14

BELMARSH PRISON, WOOLWICH

'Your name's Ian Campbell?'

Her seventh patient that day nodded. He had been ushered into the room by an officer who then went and sat outside the closed door. The patient was thin, fair-haired and good-looking in a boyish way, and maybe, she thought, in a slightly girlish way too. Gay? Perhaps. He was also very young. Indeed the file in front of her confirmed he was just eighteen and that he was on remand for shoplifting. Why he had robbed a shop was also obvious from her notes. Like so many in Belmarsh, he had a drug problem and also, like them, the money from petty crime was the only way to feed his addiction. Probably crack-cocaine – that had the worst craving.

'How are you?'

'Och, terrible, Miss.' Quite a strong Scottish accent – evident in only three words.

'Because of withdrawal?'

'Nah, I can get drugs here. No problem.'

After only three weeks working in this place, Alice was surprised by very little.

'What, then?'

'I think I'm in danger.'

'Danger? What kind of danger?'

Her patient sighed. She was alarmed to see that he was close to tears.

'On our block, there's this man. A horrible one. I dunno what he's in for, but it must be serious. Almost a lifer. He seems to have lots of influence, power. All the other cons are scared of him and I bet he's got some of the screws, the officers, fixed as well. He has a cell with a bit of luxury, and all the best tracksuits and trainers, so I've heard. Loads of money.'

Alice tried to hide her sudden interest.

'What's he look like?'

'Bloody big, shaven-headed, moustache and covered in tattoos. Like that Bronson fella they made a film about.'

Alice knew he wasn't talking about Charles Bronson, the Hollywood actor, but someone who'd taken his name, and one famous at Belmarsh, and several other prisons as Britain's most violent and difficult prisoner. Exactly like the man she wanted to find out about.

'So what's his name?' She guessed she already knew.

'MacDonald, Miss. Dunno his first name. Everyone calls him Big Mack.'

Alice realized that, by complete chance, she might be close to finding out more about the man they suspected. She disguised her excitement by writing in her notebook.

'So what's your problem with this Big Mack?' she asked calmly. 'You're on remand. You shouldn't be here for very long.'

'I'll tell you, Miss. He's taken a shine to me. Three days ago, he comes over during 'Association', you know, when we're not banged up and we're allowed to mix with other cons.'

Alice nodded.

'And he says he fancies me. In fact, he says, 'Laddie, I'm going to rape you and I'm going to *enjoy* raping you, you fockin' Campbell.'

The young man whimpered for a moment, as if about to cry. 'And he *did*, he *did*!'

Alice couldn't help patting his arm, despite the fact that touch wasn't normally allowed. 'What did he mean by that – you know, the Campbell thing?'

Slumped over, he sniffled, 'Dunno. I suppose something about Glencoe, but it was probably just an excuse – or his idea of a sick joke.'

Alice suddenly realized he was talking about the infamous murderous attack in a glen of the Scottish Highlands on the MacDonalds by the Campbells, to whom they'd given hospitality – the so-called 'Massacre of Glencoe' – a byword for treachery.

'But that *must* be three hundred, four hundred years ago,' she said, astonished.

'Aye, but some MacDonalds still remember it. I've even seen office doors in Scotland with "NO CAMPBELLS TO ENTER HERE" written on them. But for Big Mack, it was probably only an excuse to go for me.'

He looked up and stared at Alice with a look of desperation.

'Anyway, Miss, you've *got* to get me moved from that block. And fast. Before anything worse happens. Christ, I've got a girlfriend waiting for me on the outside. That's why I pretended to be a bit mad. And there's something else.' He looked nervously towards the closed door.

'What?'

'The bastard threatened me. Said he'd 'jug' me if I complained.'

'*Jug* you? What does that mean?'

'You ought to know. They hold you down and pour a jug of boiling water over your face, mixed with sugar. Disfigures you for life.'

Alice stared at him, shocked to the core.

'And then he said that if I told my folks in Aberdeen, he'd do them too. He said he knew how to kill people on the out, no problem.'

Like, for instance, Robin, the senior police officer who'd put him inside, thought Alice, grimly.

'Okay, I'll ask your Block Governor to move you at once, and I'll fix to see you again on Friday, same time.'

||||||

They never learn not to blab, do they? Stupid boy. As if I wouldn't find out.

||||||

'I'm afraid Campbell won't be coming this morning, Dr Diamond.' The male nurse looked sheepish, running through the list of her appointments.

'Why not? He was my top priority.'

'I'm afraid he's gone.'

'Gone? Where? What, to another prison?'

'I suppose so. I dunno. They told me he was moved in the middle of the night.'

So she had been able to save the boy. But probably only just in time. She only just managed to concentrate enough to get through the rest of the interviews of the day, as one thought plagued her. Campbell's sudden removal would have meant that Mack must also have guessed to *whom* he had talked. Alice began to realize the terrible danger *she* was now in. Suddenly Belmarsh took on the sinister feel for her that it must have for all its prisoners. The oppressive corridors, the miserable locked cells, the slamming of the barred gates, the constant clinking of the officers' keys. All at once, she couldn't wait to get outside, as if she were a prisoner herself.

As darkness fell, she stumbled across the car park, a small, hunched and frightened figure, and slumped into the seat of her friendly and familiar GTI. She stared at the looming bulk of the prison through the windscreen. It had begun to rain.

After a while, she started the engine, turned on the wipers and eased the car out into the evening traffic. She would never go back, she *must* never go back. And she would have to think of a plausible excuse why not. And explain her abject failure to Robin and Tim. They were right. She'd been a fool, an utter fool.

||||||

After a miserable hour in the rush hour traffic of rain-soaked south London, and back in her big old house in Putney, she resisted the temptation to have one of the cigarettes she'd stashed for real emergencies. But she had no hesitation about a really stiff drink, a vodka and tonic – with almost more vodka than tonic.

Her first call was to Robin Marshal. She asked him if he was alone, which he was, to her relief.

'Yup. Pam's just been put to bed by her carer.'

'Are you okay, Robin?'

'Not too bad, considering.'

'Really glad to hear it.' She paused.

'Remember the boy at Belmarsh I told you about, the Campbell kid? The one who was in real danger from Mack?

'Sure.'

'Well, I got him moved. Probably only just in time.'

At first there was silence from Robin.

'You can't go back, Alice.'

'I know. Mack will realize who the boy talked to. I've already emailed my resignation pleading a health problem. It's time to think about ourselves. It certainly looks as if it could be MacDonald behind the attack on you. And that he'll stop at nothing. And with publicity about Hammond, he'll quickly work out my links to you.'

She paused.

'My God, Robin, who would have thought that you had to be more afraid of someone *after* they'd been locked up. And *please* don't tell me you told me so.'

'Hard not to. You've been an idiot, Alice. Brave, but an idiot.'

Alice smarted. Robin was right, although she'd done it on his behalf.

'Anyway, let's get together with Tim to talk things over. I'm happy to come down to you. Perhaps this weekend, if Tim can get off. I'll call him next.'

||||||

James MacDonald, 'Big Mack', sat quietly on his bed and thought very carefully.

In many ways, he *did* resemble the so-called 'most dangerous prisoner in Britain', Charles Bronson. He, too, was shaven-headed, with a moustache, heavily muscled and tattooed. But the resemblance stopped there. Bronson was extremely, often mindlessly, violent and disruptive, first jailed for a bungled shotgun robbery of a Post Office that had netted him just £26 and a seven-year jail sentence. Since then, he had been moved from prison to prison, his sentence increasing every time he'd assaulted a prison officer or a fellow inmate. He'd become famous enough – they'd even made a film about him – but his way of doing things was certainly not 'Big Mack's' style.

MacDonald's career of criminal violence was actually much more dangerous. Brought up by a single mother in the high-rise slums of Glasgow, he had half-killed another kid at sixteen in a vicious quarrel over drug territory. Two years later another youth had disappeared, but nobody had been able to prove his involvement. He was now in Belmarsh for 'attempted murder', but he often smiled when he thought of the *actual* murders for which he had never been caught.

But 'Big Mack' had decided to become a businessman. Not for him the attention-seeking antics of inmates like Bronson. It had taken him only a few days at Belmarsh to work out that he should consistently appear to be a model prisoner – at least to the guards. If he were going to take over and build up a drug business, he knew he must have the maximum freedom of movement.

The first task was to be upgraded to become an 'Enhanced' prisoner – up from 'Standard'. What he did *not* want was to be demoted down from 'Standard' to 'Basic' by *any* bad behaviour. 'Enhanced' prisoners had a room with their own television, a pool table and comfortable chairs. More important, you could have a free run of the floor, unlike other prisoners who were often locked up for many hours and only able to mingle with other prisoners during the brief hour of 'Association'.

To become 'enhanced', MacDonald had opted first to be a cleaner and then a gym instructor. He had even toyed with the notion of applying to be a 'Listener', but figured that was a step too far.

After two years, Mack had achieved a money-making empire, mostly trading in drugs, with a profitable side business in mobile phones and phone cards. He had staff on 'the take' and prisoners and their families scared, or even terrified of him. He also had half a million in several secret bank accounts. All had gone well until he started breaking his own rules.

First he had allowed his rage at that Detective Inspector Marshal, the man who'd sent him down, to get the better of him – and his attempt at revenge had then gone horribly wrong. Even more stupidly, his frustrated bisexuality had led to the Campbell incident. And *who* was that woman psychologist the wretched boy had blabbed to?

He'd soon find out.

CHAPTER 15

BIGHTON, HAMPSHIRE

When Alice pulled into the driveway of Robin's house, she noticed that another car, a grey one, Tim's, was already parked there. She rang the bell and Robin came to the door. Persistent barking came from the back of the house.

'Hello, Alice.' He kissed her cheek. 'Sorry old Benny's not here with his usual nice welcome. Since the knife attack, he's not been the same, now very suspicious of strangers.'

He smiled. 'Can't blame the poor fellow. Feel a bit like that myself.'

With Robin leaning slightly on a cane, they walked into the living room. His son, big, bluff Tim, got up with a smile to greet her. He poured coffee for them and they settled round a big glass table. Alice knew that she was looking pent-up and glum, so she decided to grasp the nettle.

'Robin, I've already told you and please don't say 'I told you so'. I admit my scheme to find out more has backfired really badly. To my horror, it nearly resulted in the death of a kid in jail, and it's almost certainly alerted that bastard to my presence and as a potential danger to him and his highly profitable set-up.'

Robin raised a hand. 'I suppose we do have one upside. At least we now know that our hunch may be right and MacDonald might be the man, or almost certainly is,' Tim intervened. 'Yes, but the problem is that we don't really know what to do about it, even if we are right. Or, indeed, whether we *should* do anything.'

'I *do* have one idea,' said Alice. 'I became quite friendly with Joe Bain's friend, the Deputy Governor who let me take up the post – Mary Bloomfield, about the same age as me. She gave me a long briefing when I first arrived, and she was pretty emphatic about the present state of prisons in general – and of Belmarsh in particular.

It was to her that I sent the message, the one that never got acted on. I called her yesterday. She couldn't talk then, but she told me to call her on her mobile at eleven today, when she'd be alone.'

She looked at her watch. 'That's in five minutes.'

'Why not call now?' asked Robin.

'Nothing to lose,' agreed Tim.

'Okay, but one thing. I don't think she'll open up if she thinks she's speaking to all of us. So please keep quiet, but listen in – I'll put it on speaker.'

A few minutes later, with a fresh coffee and a notebook in front of her, Alice reached for her iPhone, turned on the volume and dialled.

'Hello. Mary Bloomfield.'

'Hi, Mary, It's Alice.'

'Hi, Alice. I'm so sorry you're leaving us, and so suddenly. I couldn't quite understand why. Was it really because you're ill? If so, I'm sorry, and hope you're soon better. I was genuinely looking forward to having a like-minded ally around.'

'Well, you may understand in a moment. Can I ask you, did you get the two urgent messages I sent on Wednesday evening about moving that Ian Campbell from his block at once?'

'No, I only got *one* such message. Your emailed one. And I acted upon it.'

'Thank goodness, you did. He was in real danger. But it's curious because I'd sent a second message. It was a written one, entrusted to a Principal Officer.'

'And which officer was that?'

'Phillips.'

There was a pause.

'Principal Officer Phillips did something very peculiar on Thursday. He resigned, without any notice. Just left his keys and went.'

'Do you know, Mary, I'm not at all surprised.'

'Why?'

'Let me explain. Ian Campbell engineered to get himself a psychological interview because he was completely terrified. He was in tears, petrified. He said that a long-term prisoner, James MacDonald, had raped him and intended to go on doing so. MacDonald also threatened to maim or kill him if he talked about it to anyone, and do the same to anyone else on the inside or even outside if they blabbed – even people like his parents up in Aberdeen. So you see why I sent the note?'

There was a pause.

'Yes, I do. And I'll start an immediate investigation.'

'Good.' Alice paused. 'But I'll bet you right now that everyone will clam up and you'll never get to the bottom of it. He seems to be called 'Big Mack' for good reason. He's apparently really intimidating. He'll have the inmates dead scared and some of the staff bribed.'

Robin had leaned forward with a finger to his lips to try to signal to Alice that she was revealing too much interest in 'Big Mack' – and too much knowledge about him. She nodded to reassure him.

'You may be right, Alice.'

They thought they detected a sigh from Mary.

'But all I can do is try. And we'll start looking a great deal more carefully at *Mister* MacDonald. Try to reduce his power, clip his wings. Perhaps with some unexpected raids on his Block. Look, I'll get back to you on this mobile about how we get on. Okay?'

'Sure. Thanks, Mary. That's very helpful. I'll await your call. Bye.'

Alice switched off the phone and put it down. She looked at her friends, somewhat downcast.

'Well, as you could hear, I don't think that did much good. But I didn't want to push her any further, and we may be able to use her influence later.'

Robin looked very serious. 'It looks as if we'll all have to be very careful – and *all* of the time. God, I wish I were fitter, and with a nice big protective police force round me.'

'This is ridiculous!' Tim suddenly blurted out, standing up. 'Here we are, responsible citizens, serving and retired police even, and we're being threatened from *inside* a jail by a murderous maniac! It's completely out of order.'

'Maybe,' said his father, conscious that Tim was the youngest of them and had not lost all of his idealism. 'But such things are now a fact of life. With drugs, drones, crowded prisons, budget cuts and nanny-like European laws, everything's changed.

And it's no good saying things like that wouldn't have happened in our day.

Anyway, on a brighter note, I'm going to take Pam to Spain next week. We certainly need the break.'

As she drove home, Alice began to feel really quite frightened. If Robin, a big ex-senior policeman, could be knifed half to death, what might happen to a slightly-built woman living alone?

She'd better stick to John as much as possible. But for the moment she didn't want to spook him with unfounded fears and false alarms. The last time she'd got herself into this kind of trouble she'd lost him for three years.

CHAPTER 16

HASLEMERE

Astri Tibbs knew it was her son John calling. It was a mid-day ritual every Sunday, and probably too much of one she thought, knowing she'd worry if he *didn't* phone.

'Hi, Mum, how's things?'

'Fine. Pretty good. And Arthur's much better, thank God. Not nearly as breathless, and hopefully he won't need a stent. We even went for a walk up on Blackdown yesterday.'

'Gosh, not to the top, I hope!' John remembered what a hike that was in his boyhood, especially when they had to find that out-of-control and constantly disappearing Irish Setter of theirs.

'No, just a ten-minute climb from the car-park and back. The doctor said it would be good for him, and that with luck, he wouldn't need an operation.'

'Thank God for that. What a relief!'

'And how are *you*?' asked Astri.

'Okay. But I thought I'd better tell you I've bust up with Susannah.'

Astri hadn't much liked her son's girlfriend on the four occasions he'd brought her down to Haslemere for lunch, but had hidden her thoughts from him, dismayed that John had seemed oblivious to how spoiled she obviously was. A striking girl certainly, but also – in her view and that of Arthur – just as strikingly self-centred, constantly changing the subject back to herself. But perhaps John *did* notice that irritating habit, but chose to ignore it because of ample compensations of a sort that neither she nor Arthur wanted to think about.

She decided to lie. 'Oh dear, I'm sorry about that.'

'Don't be. I'm not. To be honest, I'm glad I'm out of it. I took her to the Ritz a few weeks ago on her birthday, and that was the last straw. She was so bloody dismissive about it all, and frankly, downright rude. And would you believe it, she even said I should have bought her a ring as well!'

'Good God! What, an engagement ring? What a cheek! Seems you're well shot of her. So darling, footloose and fancy-free again?'

'Not quite.' John paused, wondering what his mother's reaction would be to what he said next. Almost certainly negative. But he needed to test the water, to see how troubled it still was. Maybe, he hoped, it had calmed considerably over the past three years.

'Mum, what would you and Dad feel if got back with Alice?' It was now his mother's turn to pause.

John waited for her to respond, picturing her reaction and expecting her to sigh. But to his surprise, she didn't.

'Funny you should mention her. I was reading an article by her only yesterday when I took Arthur to the doctor. In a magazine called *Psychology Today*. In fact, I asked if I could take it home. Rather a good article, as it happens. All about recovering from major trauma. I suppose she's had more than enough experience of that.'

'She certainly has.' John was relieved to hear his mother acknowledge the nightmare Alice had been through, just as he should have done much sooner.

'So you wouldn't mind if we tried again, tested the water?' he asked tentatively.

Now came her expected sigh as Astri recalled the scandal three years before when Alice had two-timed her son – albeit very briefly – with someone who turned out to be a serial killer, David

Hammond. Ghastly for John when the news got out, but also for herself and Arthur, with the media constantly hounding them for juicy nuggets to add to an already sensational and salacious story.

'Mum, you still there?'

'Yes. Well, John – it's your life. And you must do what makes you happy, even if we aren't. You're a grown man. You don't need to ask for our approval.'

'No, but I'd rather have it. I'd hate it if we got back together and you couldn't face seeing her again. That's assuming it'll work out this time. But I suppose I'd understand.'

Another pause before Astri responded.

'Well, the last thing we'd want is to lose you because we don't approve of her.

Anyway, we don't still disapprove – or at least, not half as much. We've had three years to think about it and put it all behind us, or most of it. And we now realise she was a victim of that horrendous man. At least he's dead. And she did help catch him and stop him, I'll give her that.'

'And nearly got killed for it', added John.

Astri reached for her mug of coffee.

'Look John, if you still think you love her and she still loves you – well, we can't stand in your way. And we wouldn't want to. But for God's sake, don't rush things.'

'Thanks, Mum. The fact is that, by absolute chance, I saw her at the Ritz when I was there with Susannah, and it all came flooding back. The good times, everything we had in common. And I'm sure it was the same for her.

Unbelievably, we'd been shown to the table right next to her and the chap she was with, but I managed to get us moved. And for the rest of the evening I kept realizing my feelings for her had never really gone. Probably why I've made so many ghastly mistakes with women since we split up.'

Astri laughed. 'Not all ghastly, darling. Although, to be honest, we weren't too keen on Susannah. I can't say either of us will be in tears now she's gone.'

John smiled to himself. And his parents hadn't even seen the *really* unpleasant side of her. A lucky escape.

'John, how often have you actually *seen* Alice – since The Ritz?'

'Once or twice. And enough to know there's still something there. In fact, a lot. For me, at least. And probably for both of us.'

Astri sighed.

'Well then, the best of luck. But take care, John. It's not always wise to go back to the past, revisiting old wounds and dredging up ancient grievances. And to be honest, darling, if she could cheat on you once, couldn't she do that again?'

'I don't think so. Not now.'

John suddenly heard his father's voice in the background. Normally his mother would have handed him the phone, but this time she didn't.

'Sorry, I've got to go,' she told him, suddenly switching off her mobile.

'Was that John?' asked Arthur.

'Yes, but he was in a frightful hurry.'

'Everything okay with him?'

'Fine,' replied Astri, deciding this was not the time to reveal their son's news.

||||||

Alice's landline rang.

'Hi, it's me.'

'Hi, John.'

'Look, I wonder if you'd like to come to Richmond Park next Sunday and see the model planes? And if you're not too bored, you might want to see the collection at my new house afterwards. I've had a shed built at the bottom of the garden, and it's now my airport. And then, if you like, we could go somewhere local for lunch. I'd also appreciate some new ideas for the garden. It's a right old mess.'

'Glad to be of help, and the airport sounds fun.'

John laughed. First girlfriend who'd said that!

'Great. What if I pick you up on my way to Richmond – at about ten?'

'Fine. See you then.'

CHAPTER 17

HASLEMERE

Just before six am when the 'Farming Today' programme had given way to the rather eccentric British tradition, the birdsong of that morning's 'Tweet of the Day', Arthur was eagerly waiting for the news, with a catch-up on the impressive Tory gains starting the night before. But Astri's mind was certainly not on the news and what the BBC Four commentators were about to say.

She patted Arthur's hand. 'Arthur, I need to talk to you. Could you switch that off?'

'What, *now*? Aren't you interested in the results?'

'Not right now. No.'

Click.

Arthur turned to Astri. 'Okay, what is it?'

After forty years of marriage he knew her well enough to know that only something serious would interrupt her interest in the news, and especially during elections. And he'd noticed that she'd been unusually quiet for two or three days, not like her at all.

'Right, what's bugging you?'

'John.'

'What about him?'

'He's seeing Alice again.'

A pause. 'Really? How do you know?'

'He told me when he phoned on Sunday. I didn't want to worry you. And I guess I thought it might go away, like a bad dream. But I can't keep it in any longer. A trouble shared, as they say.'

Arthur pondered for a while.

'Maybe not such a bad dream. Frankly, I think she had far more going for her than any of the girls he's met since, or even before. Or at least the ones we know about. And they were maybe the better ones. Probably why none of them lasted.'

'But Arthur, after all we've been through, you surely don't want them to get back together?'

'If it makes John happy, yes.'

'So that's it then, is it? We just wait for the worst.'

Arthur paused. 'Or best. And if it's the best for John, we'll have to learn to accept it.'

'But how *can* it be the best? A girl once involved with a serial murderer, and just how involved we'll never know? A girl whose face was splashed all over the papers and the TV, and making our lives – and John's – unutterable hell?'

'Astri, *think*! If John can forgive her, we can too. And what was it? Two or three dates at most, if I remember. Didn't you ever double date someone?'

'No, I don't think I did. And if I did, I certainly wouldn't have slept with them both.' She sighed. 'So we just sit here, and wait for it all to happen again?'

'Astri, *listen* to me. The chances of getting involved with a killer like Hammond are a million to one. And if John's accepted what happened and forgiven Alice, that's surely proof he still loves her – and probably a damned sight more than all those other girls. We'll have to learn to accept what happened too. And start again.'

'Well, I'm not sure I can.'

'You can, and you will. As *I* will, if it all works out. *Think*, darling. Think of all those girlfriends. One bust-up after another. Three years wasted time.'

'Well, I hardly think Alice will want to see *us* again. So if they do get together, that's it. Or it'll be just John on his own, coming here out of duty, resenting us.'

'No, it won't.' He was getting a little irritated by her stubborn pessimism, and rather wanted to get back to the news. 'If she still loves John, she'll make the effort for him. As *I* will. And as *you* will, too. As you must.'

'So we just gaily forget the past, as if it never happened?'

'No, we have to learn to forgive. And if we don't, we'll have a very unhappy son. That's if it lasts this time. And I've got a curious feeling it might.'

Both were silent for a while, thinking about the past, the trial of David Hammond, the lurid newspaper articles, and the ghastly media intrusion into their lives.

Astri shook her head. 'Arthur, sometimes I don't believe you.'

'Nor me, you. But one thing I *do* believe – if you'd had a fling with someone else, I'd have forgiven you.'

'But I'd hardly have had a fling with a serial killer.'

'Astri, Alice didn't know he *was*. And it was only two dates with him, as far as I remember.'

'Two too many.'

'Look, I'm going downstairs for a cup of coffee. And while I'm there, have a real think. Above all, think of losing our only son, as we will if we don't accept it. That's if it lasts this time, as it probably will. Any relationship that can survive such trauma has something going for it. In fact, far more than something.'

Astri suddenly knew he was right – at least on that last point. And that if John and Arthur could forgive Alice and brush the past aside, she would have to learn to do that too.

'Anyway,' smiled Arthur, 'you stay here, and I'll bring up a coffee. And turn the radio on again. At least it's good news, well, if you're a Tory. I'm not sure I am these days. Frankly, I'm not sure about anything any longer.'

'Nor me. Join the club.'

CHAPTER 18

PUTNEY

It was dark outside, the end of a long working day, as Maggie came into Alice's consulting room with an armful of files. She looked worried.

'Did you hear the doorbell ring just now?'

'No, can't say I did. Must have been concentrating. Who was it?'

'One of those people selling stuff door to door, probably unemployed or just out of prison. Odd time to come. Bit weird. People don't like strangers coming in the dark.'

Alice sighed. 'Bless him, but I hope you told him we didn't want anything. I've got a cupboard full of useless dusters for being soft-hearted with people like that. I do feel sorry for them, but I don't need any more junk. And you can always give them a quid or two from that pot in the hall.'

'They don't like that – charity. Not without selling anything. Anyway, I did send him away nicely. And the odd thing was, he didn't seem terribly keen to sell me anything in the first place. Normally, they try and persuade you, suddenly fishing out dishcloths and things and their ID cards and pleading their case. But this one didn't. He just zipped up the bag, cool as a cucumber, smiled politely and left.'

'So?'

'I was worried. There was something rather strange, unusual about him. It's out-of-work teens normally, or people in their twenties – out of youth programmes. But this chap was big and confident. And in his thirties. Didn't look the part at all.'

Maggie put down the files.

'So I'm afraid I did something I'd *never* normally do. When he left, I went to the corner window of the hall and sneaked a look through a crack in the curtain.

And there he was, taking *photos* with his mobile phone. He didn't use a flash, but your security lights give plenty of light. He took pictures of your car and the front door, then put away his phone and marched straight off – not to go and sell next door, just off and towards the Common.'

Alice sat still as a post.

'Now I ask you, Alice, how many salesmen take *photos*? A bit weird to say the least – as if he was sassing the joint, as they say in American films.' Maggie paused, suddenly hesitant. 'I hope you don't mind me mentioning it.'

'Of course not, Maggie. You're dead right to.' She reached for the phone, and dialled the familiar number.

'Oh God, I hope we're not going to have policemen living here again.'

'Detective-Sergeant Tim Marshal, please.'

||||||

In the event, it was agreed that a policeman *should* be stationed in the house. But not immediately, because Alice had planned a short visit to her father in France, deciding to drive rather than fly because she enjoyed the country's uncluttered roads, although she knew she'd enjoy them less while worrying about things back at home. Someone had once explained to her that while France and Britain had the same number of cars, vans and trucks, France was over three times bigger and that certainly showed, especially in the countryside. She could go for miles without seeing another car at all.

Having confirmed the trip with her father, who was more than delighted with the news, Alice booked the ferry from Newhaven to Dieppe – less driving distance in France than going through the Channel Tunnel and a shorter sea journey than sailing to Caen.

Newhaven turned out to be a bore, with no restaurants that she could spot as she drove round it, except for a McDonald's that, in the circumstances, she had no wish to visit – not with that name. She'd have to get a sandwich on the ferry, a rather boring start to what would otherwise be a much-needed break.

||||||

After four hours driving from Dieppe, Alice had reached the valley of the Loire, once again marvelling at its magnificent châteaux every few miles alongside the river. She had good friends who lived in an old house among the vineyards outside Saumur, a town with its own great château, but also once a military centre best-known for its old cavalry school and nowadays for its tank museum – a visit to which Alice had endured once or twice, careful to hide that from her hosts, Gordon and his wife Evelyne.

After a splendid dinner with them in a restaurant near the old cavalry barracks, she thankfully slept soundly for eight hours before setting off again along the Loire valley, and turning south at Vierzon. Her GTI lapped up the miles at a steady ninety most of the way, and at about four in the afternoon, just after crossing Norman Foster's magnificent necklace-like Millau Bridge, she turned off the A75 Autoroute and slowed down, crossed a bare scrub-covered plateau and then twisted down along the mountain roads and hairpins into the wooded Cévennes. At last she pulled up outside her father's old farmhouse at about five-thirty.

Harold Diamond was delighted to see his daughter and they sat on the terrace in the warmth of the evening – sipping wine as the sun began to set behind the mountain range. Alice noticed that most of the geraniums had miraculously survived the bitter cold in February and that the garden was bursting with flowers – as were the roadsides leading up to the house – a wild-flower paradise.

Her father looked really well, suntanned, but older with his hair now completely white. Was that the result of the court case and the scandal of three years ago? Alice put that thought out of her mind as they decided to go out for supper, to the Auberge Cigaloise, the only hotel in St Hippolyte, and with the best food in town.

As she drove down the hill, she noticed an empty car parked by the side of the road, a blue Vauxhall Astra with British number plates, finding that curious. Apart from her father, who had a French car, there were hardly any English people in the area, and certainly none living in the houses up this narrow road – at least, as far as she knew.

But she forgot about it as she chatted to her father, catching up with his news. He told her he'd be coming over to England after the summer, because the town's Blériot replica plane club had once again been invited to come to a big vintage aviation meeting at The Shuttleworth Collection near Biggleswade. He was needed to assist in the long drive in the towing van for the plane's trailer, and more importantly to translate for the group – few of whom spoke good, or indeed any, English.

At dinner, they saw several of his friends and moved over and joined another table for coffee. Alice figured that this was just the break she needed, though thinking it might have been more fun if John had been able to join her. She was beginning to miss him already.

All in all, it was a very pleasant few days. She visited the local Silk Museum, bought some pots from a famous store outside Anduze, went for walks to look at the wildflowers, but mainly relaxed with her father in the house and garden. But she had to get back to her patients soon – and John.

She left early in the morning and after half an hour, as she drove away west from Le Vigan, she noticed a car behind her – a blue one of the same type she'd seen near her father's house. But she lost it once she was free of the town's speed-bumps, *dos d'ânes* or 'donkeys' backs' as the French called them, and really put her foot down. Out of the valley, she now climbed into the escarpment – enjoying the huge power of her car propelling her up through the twists and turns of the mountain road.

Once on the Autoroute, she didn't drop much below a hundred, except when she was in the outskirts of towns, or slowing to pay the tolls – annoying with a right-hand drive car, which meant she had to leap out to put in her credit card, with cars sometimes honking behind her.

By the Wednesday morning, she was back in Putney ready to face her patients again. And she was pleased when John called and suggested they meet up in Bicester that Friday after he'd finished a pitch to a potential advertising client there.

CHAPTER 19

BICESTER, OXFORDSHIRE

'So you've still got the GTI.'

John smiled as he got into the dark blue car outside Bicester North Station, from where he had just seen off the rest of his advertising agency team on to the London train.

'Yup, five years old, but it can still go like a bomb. Two hundred brake horsepower, six speed gearbox, nought to sixty in six seconds *and* able to top a hundred and fifty. Not that I'd ever try that. Too many cameras around.'

'Glad to hear it!'

'I took off its 30th anniversary badge years ago, so now it looks like a bog-standard GTI, or actually to most people, an ordinary VW Golf. And it's nice you've still got your old Morgan.'

John laughed. 'Couldn't bear to part with it.'

They turned on to the A41 heading east towards Aylesbury and the 'The Lion', the Waddesdon pub where they'd booked for lunch, while John chatted about the presentation he'd just done for a food company in Bicester, which he thought had gone quite well. He explained that they were up against a small local agency and a big international one, part of the giant WPP Group, and that he was a bit worried that one of his team, the youngest, might have gabbled too much and lost the momentum of the pitch. 'Anyway, we'll know in a week. Fingers crossed.'

There were several silences in the car as both had anticipated, reflecting on the past and knowing there were places not to go at the moment, and aware that a rapprochement – if possible at all – was still fragile, and they needed to go slowly. Alice was certainly not going to tell John about Robin Marshal or her time at Belmarsh – a sure way to worry him and spoil things. For now it was enough to be companionable and comfortable with each other.

And both knew the lunch date ahead would be important to them. They had met up just twice, first a week or so ago in a pub after a gap of three years, and with Liz and Phil accompanying them, so they hadn't been able to talk about much, just keeping things light. Then he had come round for supper but nothing more.

'How's your sister doing?' asked Alice, remembering Josie well, and knowing that she was about to get married to her girlfriend in Australia at the time she and John had split up.

'Fine, she's a Mum now. They adopted a little girl called Amy.'

'How lovely! And she's still in Oz?'

'Yup, Sydney.'

'And your parents, they're okay?'

'Fine, but Dad can't make it out there any more. It's a shame, but he can't take the distance. And Mum hates leaving him alone, so she won't go either. But Josie's pretty good about coming *here* once a year.'

Alice pictured Josie and her little girl, aware again that she was beginning to think about children herself, and that the man beside her was the only one she'd ever envisaged being the father. At thirty-four, she was starting to hear a clock ticking.

A few minutes later she was watching the unfamiliar road carefully. For such an important link between Oxford and Aylesbury, the A41 was a surprisingly narrow single carriageway, and very crowded on a Friday with trucks, vans and cars. It was obviously regarded as dangerous, because there was a solid 60 mph speed limit enforced by numerous yellow cameras.

Only occasionally did the busy road spread out on to brief dual carriageway sections, and it was coming up to one of them that Alice was relieved that she could let a silver BMW overtake her. It seemed to have been following far too closely for a couple of miles.

The BMW duly pulled out, but curiously did not overtake.

Instead, it drew alongside.

Puzzled, Alice glanced sideways.

To her sudden horror, the back window of the BMW was open *and someone masked was aiming a gun straight at her.*

A sudden instinct made her floor the accelerator, and the GTI growled and shot forward. She heard a rattle of shots, and something hitting the back of her car.

'*Jesus!*' exclaimed John, who'd been looking the other way – oblivious to the threat.

Her heart rate soaring, Alice changed down and took the little car up to ninety, and as they reached the single carriageway she just managed to slide in front of a truck that now blocked the BMW. The truck driver sounded his horn furiously at her apparently reckless driving, so John's next and vitriolic words went unheard.

Driving on for a mile at way over a hundred, Alice figured that she was safely out of sight, and spotting a gap in the heavy oncoming traffic, changed down again, and turned hard right, wheels squealing, down a narrow side road through a wood. She drove fast for about three hundred yards before skidding into a farmyard cluttered with vehicles and equipment, and lurched to a stop behind an old rusting combine harvester, keeping the engine running. She was shaking all over.

'Christ!' whispered John, equally shaken. '*What the fuck was that about?*'

Alice switched off her engine, saying nothing. They both got out and Alice exhaled heavily as they walked to the rear.

'There was a man with a gun in that car. Only our acceleration stopped us getting killed.' She pointed to three holes in the GTI's rear bodywork. 'See? Just level with our heads.'

John was stunned. 'But why would anyone...'

Alice interrupted. 'I think I know.'

'For God's sake Alice, what *have* you got yourself into now?'

Inside the farmhouse, they could hear a dog starting to bark furiously.

||||||

'Where the FOCK'S she gone?' shouted the driver, as he alternated between speeding up and slowing down to look down likely-looking left turnings off the road. 'And why the hell didn't yer fire earlier, when yer had the chance, Paddy – Mister fockin' IRA hotshot?'

'Well she just shot forward as I pulled the fockin' trigger. And did yer see the *speed* of her when she took off? That's no fockin' ordinary Golf, I can tell you!'

'Shut up and calm down, my Mick friends,' said the leader in the front passenger seat, in a quiet Glasgow accent. 'Slow down and stick to the plan. We'll get to the lock-up garage in Aylesbury, alter back the number plates, pick up the empties, cover the car, change to the Audi and drive slowly back to London.

But I don't fancy being the one who has to break the news to Mack. He can be pretty unreasonable about such things.'

He stared out of the window. He didn't mind killing people, but he had a curious dislike of telling lies – however necessary.

||||||

Jimmy Bentall, the farmer, was enjoying his routine second pint at

'The Lion' at Waddesdon when he got the call.

'What's up, love? What do you mean, police? Okay, *okay*! Calm down. Hold on, I'll be right back. I'm coming.' He stuffed his phone into his pocket.

He looked up at his puzzled drinking companions.

'You're not going to *believe* this. Some girl in a car says she was about to be shot at, and she drove into my yard. And the cops are crawling all over the place. Maureen's gone hysterical!'

He reached for his glass and finished his pint.

'Right, chaps. Better go.'

||||||

Sitting in the Aylesbury headquarters of Thames Valley Police, Alice and John were being questioned by Detective Sergeant Alec Wilson. He'd just come back into the room, having checked with Joe Bain at Scotland Yard, who had clearly filled him in on her background.

'I have to say that normally around here, faced by a driver telling us that a gun had been fired at her from another car, we might be just a tad sceptical. However, that Detective Inspector at Scotland Yard has more than vouched for you, Dr Diamond.' He paused, looking at her with evident surprise. 'I gather guns have been pointed at you before.'

Alice nodded.

He sat down. 'We've not got much to go on. Our CCTV trawl, including the speed cameras, has revealed *some* shots of your car and the BMW. But there were no more sightings of the BMW after Aylesbury. All three rounds that hit your car were badly deformed. We *may* get something off them, but I rather doubt it. They were small, nine mill, which is why they squashed up against German steel.' He shook his head. 'It may sound callous, but it would be easier for us if they'd hit you – you know, from an evidence point of view. No offence meant.'

'None taken.' Alice was used to such gallows humour from police colleagues. John, frowning, was clearly not.

'Those were no kids, trying to scare you. Or thieves, or carjackers. We think they may have been the real thing – professionals. Without your violent acceleration, they'd have got you. So we *don't* think they'll be driving around in that BMW waiting to be spotted by us. They'll have hidden it, changed it or even chopped it. And probably just a few hundred yards from here. Then they probably went off in a back-up vehicle.'

Alice and John had a long debrief all afternoon with DS Wilson. They'd been given some sandwiches, which Alice ruefully thought were really not much of a substitute for the romantic gourmet meal they'd been so looking forward to in Waddesdon.

Alec Wilson's parting words were hardly reassuring, 'If this is not a random incident, or one of mistaken identity, you may still be in danger. In my view, you probably need police protection. You'd get it here, but I can't vouch for the Met with all their budget cuts. We'll certainly be investigating it as attempted murder, and we'll keep you informed on progress.'

He sighed heavily. 'Of course, we'll inform you immediately if anything comes up.'

'Thanks,' Alice nodded, but his words were scant comfort.

It was early evening before they could get back in her car and set off back to London. Halfway there, Alice noticed a little pub, and they decided to break the journey, not that either of them felt much like food. But a drink was certainly what they needed.

Over a glass of wine, Alice began to explain the dangerous situation that she and Robin Marshal appeared to be in and their suspicions about the mysterious 'Big Mack' and Belmarsh Prison.

To her surprise, and despite his shock, John actually appeared very understanding and concerned – a great relief. He'd gone through so much before – as she had – and she greatly feared that the incident might wreck their relationship all over again. But he *did* express his deep worries, only natural in the circumstances.

'To be honest, Alice, I really *do* wish you'd stay out of police work, at least the sort you seem to do. It's incredible we can't even go out for a quiet lunch together without this sort of thing happening. For God's sake, we could both be *dead* by now. You don't seem to realize that. Can't you just run a *normal* psychology practice without all this? I don't know about you, but I don't think I can face any more horrors like that, and always worrying about you and what you're up to – and to be honest, what you're afraid of telling me. The idea of your girlfriend getting shot is, well, horrific, and it's not much better to know she's being stalked at home, like by that man who came round to sell you things and took photos.'

'*Girlfriend*?' Alice was suddenly pleased to be considered that again, but acutely aware it couldn't go on like this, constantly fearing for him as well as herself. Police work would have to go, she suddenly realized, that's if she were ever able to have a normal relationship and be able to discuss day-to-day things freely.

'I'm truly sorry.'

John shook his head. 'But maybe not sorry enough to change.'

'I am now. I don't want to have to watch my back all the time any more than you do.'

John smiled. 'Glad to hear it.' He picked up his glass and clinked it against hers. 'So here's to a quieter life, if we're allowed to live one.'

But it was about to be exactly the opposite.

Suddenly, just as they were getting their coats on, Alice's mobile rang. She sat down again.

It was Robin Marshal calling, very unexpectedly – from Spain.

CHAPTER 20

ESTEPONA, SOUTHERN SPAIN

Robin and Pam had been really looking forward to their holiday. Of course, it was not just to be in the sun again, but also to get away from Britain and the ever-present menace it seemed to pose for them. Robin had recovered pretty well from the knife attack, but was still nowhere near feeling his old self.

Their plane had swept over Gibraltar in magnificent weather and touched down on the very short runway, always a slightly tense moment. And every year, as night follows day, Robin would say, 'Not half as bad as the old Hong Kong airport. You could look straight into the windows of the Walled City. And almost see what people were eating.' Pam found it amusing that he repeated himself so reliably, almost word for word.

Then, in Jim Fawcett's big Mercedes, with the wheelchair in the back, they had left behind the border with Gibraltar, driven through the cork trees along the old coast road, passed the guarded gates of ultra-smart Sotogrande, crossed the Guadiaro River bridge and were now approaching Estepona. Robin smiled as he reflected on a real irony. Unsurprisingly in view of its superb climate, Spain's Costa del Sol was home to thousands of foreign residents – and many from Britain. And what he thought more surprising, and rather ironic, is that there were two very different types living so close together, retired British policemen – and retired British crooks and villains on the run.

One of the reasons the Marshals liked Estepona was that it was one of the few towns on that ever more popular and crowded coast to have kept at least some of its old charm, with its whitewashed houses crowding narrow streets, its little harbour and unspoiled beaches. And two hundred metres from the sea there was a small complex of bungalows almost entirely populated by retired or still serving British policemen and women. So it was not surprising that the Marshals had been going there for years, always staying with their good friends Jim and Sheila Fawcett, who had been among the first to buy there.

Like Robin, Jim had served in the Met and had also risen to the rank of Chief Inspector before retiring, but unlike many of his less enterprising Estepona neighbours, had decided to take Spanish lessons as soon as he arrived, as had his wife. As a result, he and Sheila had good Spanish friends and enjoyed a much fuller life than most of the other ex-pats who tended to go to the same English pub rather too often and shop in the British mini-market or at places like 'Bill's Bar' or 'Pete's Meats'.

Even when Parkinson's Disease had struck Pam, it was still a good place for them to holiday. Gibraltar was less than thirty miles away and the bungalow was perfectly suited to her needs. No stairs, a paved patio, tiled floors instead of carpets, with no gravel paths to obstruct her wheelchair – and a shower-room rather than a bathroom.

Robin was always surprised by how much harder it was to look after the disabled in England, for example, with only ten per cent of London's underground stations having lifts, and gravel drives being so popular. Not that he thought that everywhere could adapt – just too expensive. But surely, he thought, more places could make an effort – although it would come too late for Pam.

Within minutes of their arrival, they were sitting looking out over the communal swimming pool and the mountain beyond, and soon after, Sheila had started preparing lunch. It was hot but pleasantly quiet, being too early in the season for the schools to have broken up. So no children, just one old chap doing rather slow lengths of breaststroke. Pam had a glass of Valdepeñas white wine, although she drank with a straw, because her hands shook a little. Robin nursed a San Miguel.

'I thought you might like to take it quietly today,' said Jim, also drinking a beer. He'd noticed how frail Pam had become since last year.

'Good idea,' said Robin. 'Even with wheelchair assistance, the distances at Gatwick are a bit of a nightmare. But it was good to have someone else to push Pam. I'm still a bit wounded and not up to any distance.'

'Then tomorrow,' continued Jim, 'we thought we'd meet up for lunch with the Dennys in a new place on the road to Casares, if that's okay with you two.'

'Fine, we're in your hands. It'll be good to see them again.' He looked around, appreciatively.

'I must say Jim, it's really great to be here – and for a whole fortnight. I hope we're not too much trouble.'

'Don't be silly. It's always great to have you. And, let's face it, you and Pam need the break.'

He looked up to see his wife approaching. 'Ah, lunch – and Sheila's gaspacho. She remembered how much you liked it last time!'

||||||

Days later they were still having a good time, a pleasant mixture of seeing old friends like the Dennys and then going further afield with a drive up into the mountains to Ronda. Robin was now able to do about twenty lengths of the pool, adding a few more each day.

His main scar from the stab wound had largely healed, although he obeyed the hospital's orders not to let the fierce Spanish sun get to it, covering it carefully with a daily dressing.

It was on the Sunday evening that everything changed.

With Mike and Sharon Denny, they had all gone for 'tapas' at a nearby bar and were walking down a quiet street in the semi-darkness, with Robin pushing Pam's wheelchair. There was a sudden engine noise, and they all looked round. With no lights on, a SEAT estate car was coming at them fast, headed straight at Robin.

'CHRIST!'

He hurled Pam's wheelchair to the right and dived to the left, groaning with pain from his recent wounds. The car just missed them both and ploughed into a wall, its radiator erupting in a cloud of steam.

Robin staggered up to look at Pam, whose wheelchair was now on its side with her still strapped in.

With supreme difficulty, and aching ribs, he hauled it upright – and stroked her hair to calm her. She was whimpering – confused, terrified and wide-eyed.

'Pam, you're okay. You'll be alright. *Pam, do you hear me?*'

Sheila intervened, noticing his desperation.

Jim was a very big man indeed. Six foot four, he had boxed for the police and had no doubt that this was no accident. He strode to the wrecked car and hauled the driver out while Robin did his best to do the same with the passenger, fortunately small, confused and frightened, and muttering in Spanish. The driver, however, was now snarling '*Shit, shit, shit!*' He was obviously British, and youngish with a face blotched by too much sun.

'What's your fucking game, sonny?' shouted Jim, holding him by the collar.

'I'm sayin' nuffink!' grunted his prisoner.

'Oh dear, look what the windscreen's done to you.' *Bang!* Jim had hit him very hard in the face. 'And the steering-wheel.' *Bang!* He'd now hit him in the ribs. 'And the gear lever.' Another blow to his body.

'So, mate, what's your game?' He raised his massive fist again.

'*Stop, STOP!* Somebody paid me, I dunno who. Someone else followed your pal from Gibraltar and I was told to meet that Miguel in Malaga, come down 'ere and he'd find the geezer I was meant to hit.'

'So you don't know who paid?'

'No, but my pal talked about McDonalds or summat.'

Robin had seen to it that Pam was safely with Sheila, and had come to stare at the driver, dragging the little Spaniard with him. A curious crowd was now coming down the street, and in the distance was the sound of a police siren.

Robin now leaned forward.

'I'm sure attempted murder will get you years in a Spanish jail. But, we'll make a deal. You get a message to whoever sent you and tell him to lay off. Or there'll be *real* trouble. And, as a gesture, we'll let you and your nasty little Spanish friend go. Okay?' He hissed again, 'okay?'

Just at that moment, a Guardia Civil sergeant forced his way though the crowd.

'Buenas tardes, Sargento Lopez,' smiled Jim, who plainly knew him well. His knowledge of Spanish and friendliness with the locals was about to pay off.

'Un accidente, sin duda. El pobre está herido. The poor boy is hurt.'

Then he added, 'Pueden ser los frenos, Enrique?'

Jim was rather pleased with his suggestion that the brakes might have been faulty. Someone had tried that ruse on him in the Commercial Road twenty years ago.

Robin Marshal was now drinking something much stronger than beer or wine and was visibly worried. Doctor Saurez had come to check up on Pam and they had put her to bed. Sheila had then gone to bed too, and Jim was putting some plaster on his knuckles.

'Whoever it is, is still after me – even out *here*, for God's sake!' Robin put down his glass, wearily shaking his head.

'And clearly they took the time and trouble to tail us from Gatwick, then all the way through the Gibraltar border to here. Following someone in a wheelchair made it even easier, I suppose. Bloody frightening, to say the least.'

'Do you have any ideas?'

'Yes, with the help of Joe Bain, you remember him, and others like my son Tim, we looked into any cases where people might have really wanted revenge. Lots of them were dead or ill or whatever. But one's in Belmarsh, a very nasty fellow – MacDonald, called 'Big Mack', someone I helped put away. It could be him.'

'Didn't that chap tonight say something about McDonalds?'

'Christ! You're right. He bloody well did!'

'Well, I'm sure you're okay out here now.'

Robin reached for his drink. Then he frowned.

'Maybe, I'm not sure. There's something else.'

'What?'

'You remember that girl in the Hammond case?'

Sure, Alice somebody.'

'Yes, Alice Diamond. A good friend, and we both went through hell over that Hammond bastard. He even tried to kill her.'

'I know. Bloody awful.'

'When I was stabbed and we all began to piece together this 'Big Mack' thing, Alice decided to volunteer for a fill-in psychologist stint at Belmarsh. Ostensibly, to check things out. I thought it was dangerous and stupid and tried to stop her, but I was very weak then and she's really headstrong, *too* headstrong. So, with Joe Bain's help through someone he knew, she went there and started work, and within a week one of her young patients seemed scared and began to talk about what 'Big Mack' had done to him and threatened to do to him and others, even on the outside. Next thing, Alice, not before time, got anxious and pulled out of Belmarsh. But it may have been too late. That Mack guy might be on to her. And as soon as he knew her name, he'll have been on to the link with me in a flash – because of all that massive Hammond serial killer publicity. He's obviously vindictive, so she may be in danger, too. I'm not sure our warnings via those two amateur assassins will really warn him off. I'm getting really worried.'

He suddenly looked at his watch. 'It's not late in England, only nine o'clock. I think I'd better make a call.'

||||||

As soon as he got through and before he could talk about his own drama, Alice launched into what had happened to her. She was then appalled when Robin interrupted to say that someone had just tried to kill *him* as well. She listened with mounting horror to his story – made all the more shocking by the barbarity of aiming a car at someone in a wheelchair.

'How's Pam coping?'

'Not too well, understandably. Pretty shaken up. But she'll be okay. Or at least, I hope so. And what about *you*, Alice?'

'Well, bloody shaken up, like her. You're going to a nice country pub lunch and a car pulls alongside and a man points and fires a machine-gun at you? It's beyond belief.'

She then told him her own story in more detail, about which he was equally horrified. For both of them, there was little doubt of a link, despite knowing the very real dangers of jumping to conclusions, naturally very discouraged in police work. But it was just too much of a coincidence.

'We'd better meet up as soon as you get back, Robin.'

'I agree. Keep Tuesday free, and I'll call you as soon as I land.'

||||||

After a full twenty minutes, Robin put down his phone and turned to Jim Fawcett, who had been trying to follow the gist of the conversation, only being able to hear Robin's side.

'You won't *believe* this, Jim. They've only gone and tried to kill Alice as well.'

'*What*? And who's they?'

'Someone tried to machine-gun her on a country road, for Christ sake – her and her old boyfriend. Thank God, she out-accelerated them and got away. She's been with the Thames Valley detectives all day.'

He paused, thinking fast.

'Do you think your Civil Guard friend has let those people go?'

'Probably not. It usually takes hours in Spain to process a traffic accident. So they might still be there.'

'Call him now. Tell him to hold them after all. This whole thing is getting out of control and we need to find out a lot more.'

Jim picked up the phone and tapped in a familiar number.

'Buenas noches. El Sargento Lopez, por favor.'

A pause. Then a request for his name.

'Si. De parte del Señor Fawcett, Jaime Fawcett. Si, el Inglés. Gracias, Señorita.'

Jim waited.

'Enrique? Buenas noches, mi amigo. Los dos del accidente – están con vosotros todavia? Bueno. Hay complicatiónes importantes, muy importantes. Por favor, detenga a los dos para la noche. Son muy peligrosos.'

Jim talked in rapid Spanish for a few minutes more and then put down his phone.

'Good. Enrique will keep them in and we can go down in the morning and do some questioning of our own. I said we'd only just realized that yours might be a murder attempt when we heard about Alice. It certainly looks as if your Mack fellow, *if* it's him behind it, and it's still a big 'if', isn't going to be put off with any warnings from here. Whoever it is seems hell-bent on taking revenge on anyone who's harmed him or even *could* harm him.'

'Well, I always thought the bastard was really evil and pretty mad when I was putting him away. A horrible man. I think I need another drink. And, Jim, let's keep all this to ourselves for the moment. I don't want Pam any more frantic than she already is.'

'Nor Sheila, for that matter.'

||||||

That night John stayed with Alice in Putney. There was no romance, and little enough sleep for either of them, but she sensed a definite feeling of protection. He held her hand most of the night, staring at the ceiling, his mind racing with the day's events.

The next day, Alec Wilson, the Detective Sergeant from Thames Valley Police, called Alice.

'Before you left us, I had my fellows check your car. We found an electronic homing device planted under it – an expensive little thing. And we're now examining it. I don't suppose *you* put it there?'

'Of course not.'

'I thought so. And it proves there was nothing random about that attack. Someone's clearly been stalking you, Dr. Diamond. And targeting your car.'

That was when Alice suddenly remembered the blue Vauxhall in France.

||||||

Idiots! All they had to do is knock off that shrink bitch on a country road and they start making excuses about how fast her car was and how they lost her. All that's going to happen now is the bloody police chasing around – and, much worse, beginning to look at me. I'll have to do something about all this incompetence.

And silence from Spain. Surely no more screw-ups? Not on the same day!

||||||

The door of the cell creaked open, and a grim-faced Sargento Lopez stood in the doorway. Behind him was another Guardia Civil with a sub-machinegun.

Lopez bent over and shouted, 'LEVANTAROS, BASTARDOS, Y VENGAN CONMIGO!'

'What's he say?' asked Steve, scrambling to his feet.

'He says to come with him.' Miguel replied, leaving out the 'bastards' bit.

'But where?'

'A dondé vámos? asked Miguel, nervously.

'Málaga.'

'Por qué?'

'El proceso legal antes del toque.'

'Processing before court.'

'But I must be able to make a telephone call!' said Steve. He knew he urgently had to get a message to England about their failure.

Miguel translated his request, without much enthusiasm.

'No es posible,' grunted the Sergeant, 'no esta permitido. Vámonos!' He jerked his thumb towards the door.

Steve could guess what he was saying, and tried to protest.

'But it's my *right* to make a call. It's European law.'

Again, Miguel translated.

'Ustedes perdieron ese privilegio cuando intentaron matar a un policía.' Lopez almost snarled the words as he spat them out.

'What the fock's he sayin' now?'

'He say you lost right when you tried to kill police officer.'

CHAPTER 21

GATWICK AIRPORT

Because of Pam's disability, they were the last passengers off the plane, but Robin was pleased to see that one of the airport's electric vehicles was waiting for them. It whisked them past the hundreds of yards of passengers on the slow-moving travelling walkways all the way to the main South terminal. There in the arrivals area they spotted Tim, who'd taken time off work to pick them up.

'Hi Dad. Hi Mum. Thank God you're back.'

He didn't want to mention the attack on the journey to their home, not wanting to make Pam any more frightened than she already was.

But he was hard-pressed to keep sounding cheerful as he drove them to Bighton. It had been bad enough that his father had nearly been knifed to death. But people trying to kill his mother in her *wheelchair*? And Alice in her car? Tim couldn't wait to talk to his father alone.

Luckily, Pam was pretty sleepy by the time they arrived – what with hours travelling and her medication, so she elected to be taken straight up to bed. When his father returned, he looked extremely strained and worried. He poured them both a Laphroaig, a single malt whisky he normally kept for special occasions.

'Well, as you can imagine, that holiday was a bit different to say the bloody least. She may be ill, but your mother's no fool. So, after finding me half dead and then us being targeted by those bastards in Spain, the whole thing was traumatic, dreadful.

I'd promised her a nice quiet retirement. And then, all this. Horrendous.'

He went on to describe in detail exactly what had happened in Spain – the bungled attack and then the next day's session in the jail with the two prisoners.

'Turns out they'd been offered a heap of money to stage some kind of accident. The English kid was very, very stupid and a rotten driver, and the Spaniard probably just a spotter. There must have been someone else in the team to make it work, someone following from Gibraltar. But that didn't stop them bungling it.

The ones in jail were both scared stiff of Jim Fawcett who'd shown how violent he could be. And the fact that he spoke Spanish and appeared pals with the Sergeant must have made them think he was paramilitary or something. Anyway, they repeated the fact that it was someone called MacDonald who'd ordered the hit and provided the cash. The stupid little Spaniard still thought that everyone was talking about the money coming from McDonalds, the hamburger chain, the only McDonalds the little prick knew. A complete moron.'

'We knew by then all about the attempted attack on Alice that same day. So we got our new Spanish police friends to up the charges and break the rules to stop any communication for as long as possible.'

Tim interrupted. 'It strikes me that stopping or cutting down communication would seem to be a vital step in corralling Big Mack. It's just ridiculous that mobile phones are as normal in jail as drugs are.'

Robin nodded and went to his desk in the corner of the room and unlocked a drawer. He came back with a pistol in his hand.

'*Jesus*, Dad, what's that?'

'Something I hope I'll never use. A point two five Beretta, the one James Bond was told to give up in that film *Dr No*. I just wanted you to know I'd got it.'

Tim frowned. 'But do you have a Firearms Licence for it? And I thought nobody in Britain was allowed handguns anyway.'

'No, Tim, I do *not* have a licence. Are you going to arrest me?'

Tim shook his head, smiling. 'Hardly. And I expect ex-Chief Inspectors might be treated more leniently than others if they found you with a pistol. And I can guess why you've got it.' He reached for the bottle. His father also helped himself to a small measure of the Laphroaig.

'The situation seems completely out of control. Here we are, law-abiding citizens, and we can be attacked all over the place on the whim of some maniac – probably in one of our jails. And there doesn't seem to be much we can do about it. Well, the very *least* I can do is quietly arm myself to protect your Mum and me.'

'Yes, but what about Alice?'

'Yes, that's been worrying me too. Alone in that big house, on a common, a bit isolated. She seems to be getting back with that boyfriend, but what's *he* meant to do? He's a civilian, an advertising man – not an SAS trooper. We'll have to get back to that Mary woman at the prison. There *must* be some pressure we can put on that bastard.'

'*If it's him,*' added Tim. 'And it's a very big 'if'. At least, far too big to risk a private vendetta. Not to mention it's entirely unprofessional.'

CHAPTER 22

WANDSWORTH

It was now several weeks later, and now that police protection had been withdrawn from Alice's house ('because of budget issues'), John was growing more and more uneasy about her living on her own again, and even working there even though Maggie was around. And he surmised, it would surely be easy enough for a stranger, and a dangerous one, to book an appointment with a psychologist. Or did people have to be referred by their GPs? He resolved to find out and confront her with his fears. If someone could aim a gun at her from a car, what *else* might they do? Not a day now went by that wasn't filled with worry. And it was getting harder and harder for either of them to concentrate on work, or enjoy anything, let alone sex.

He had never heard Alice having nightmares before, but now he was often woken in bed beside her as she re-lived the shooting incident, sometimes screaming out loud. And she was not easily calmed, instead getting up at ungodly hours, as he then did, joining her in the kitchen for a coffee.

And, of course, that was now affecting everything, He couldn't relax, any more than she could.

They were now having supper in the kitchen in his flat.

'Alice, look, we've got to do something. We can't just plough on as if nothing's happened. Especially now that policeman's gone from your house. And why the hell *has* he gone?'

'I told you. Money, probably. The usual reason. Bloody budget cuts!'

John shook his head. 'Not a good enough one. And I hate seeing you frightened and having nightmares all the time. *And* you're losing weight. For God's sake, come and *live* here, and then, and only if you really have to, go to work at your place. But frankly I think you should give up work for a bit.'

Alice said nothing for a moment.

'And do what? Sit around here all day, and put you in danger, too? I've done that once already.'

'I don't think either of us have a choice, really.'

Tears suddenly filled her eyes, which she quickly brushed away. Then shoving her plate aside, she looked at him for a while. John noticed that once again she'd hardly eaten a thing.

Now he pushed his own plate away and came round to her side of the table, his arms outstretched.

'Here.'

Alice got up and he gave her a cuddle – stroking her hair, rocking her to and fro and feeling her wet cheek against his own.

Suddenly, his mobile rang. John groaned. 'Damn, better answer it.'

Alice re-filled her glass, not listening, thinking about spending more nights at John's place. And probably days as well.

'Well, at least *that's* good news,' said John, clicking off his mobile.

'What?' asked Alice.

'That was Dad, asking us down to lunch this Sunday week.'

Alice flinched. Far from being good news, it was actually the *last* thing she wanted to hear.

Life was enough of a strain already. She suddenly pictured Astri looking at her across the table and thinking behind her face. And not with pleasant thoughts. The whole thing would be unbearable.

'Sorry, but I'm not sure I could face it right now.'

'Of course, you could. They're clearly trying to build bridges. And they did like you – a lot.'

'Once,' Alice laughed.' But they've had plenty of time to change their minds since then. And I'm not a psychologist for nothing. Grudges don't disappear that easily, if ever. And how many parents could cope with a girlfriend or boyfriend once connected with a notorious murderer? There'll always be questions hanging in the air. A huge divide, even if they wanted to cross it.'

She knew, even as the words were out of her mouth, that if she refused to go, it would drive a wedge between her and John. In the end, she had no choice – if she wanted to keep him.

'Let me think about it. Perhaps it's just a rotten time to ask me.'

'Okay, but don't wait too long. I'll have to let them know in a day or so.'

A day or so?

Alice flinched.

CHAPTER 23

CENTRAL LONDON

'Sarah Shaw.'

Alice had called the new mobile number that Sarah had given her.

'Hi. It's me.'

'Alice! Great to hear from you!' Sarah was not just being polite. After all, her scoop on the whole Hammond drama three years ago had led to her promotion and made her name as a crime reporter. She had kept the file and she and Alice had become quite friendly, meeting up two or three times a year.

'Sarah, I wonder if we can we get together? I may have something pretty big for you.'

'Sure. Wait…. how about Thursday evening? In Soho?' She gave Alice the address of a new bar that Alice had never heard of.

||||||

Sarah wondered what Alice was going to tell her. Pretty big? Surely she couldn't have got involved with yet *another* major crime incident? She'd recently reported the trial of a woman who'd pushed her husband down the stairs to his death, and where Alice had testified, and successfully. But what on earth had she got involved with *now*? She had a bottle of rosé and two glasses at the table before Alice came in, flustered.

'Sorry I'm late. I was stupid enough to drive here. I'd forgotten parking has become such a nightmare.'

After pouring themselves wine, Sarah waited with anticipation for what Alice had to say.

'You remember Robin Marshal?'

'Of course. The Detective Inspector.'

'Well, he retired early to look after his wife, who'd been diagnosed with Parkinson's.'

'Oh, that's sad. I'm sorry to hear that.'

'Yes, I think he could have done really well if he'd stayed. Even gone to the top. Anyway, they settled down in a nice cottage in Hampshire for a quiet life, with a garden and a dog and all that kind of thing.'

Sarah waited. There was nothing 'pretty big' in this story so far. But she was about to get a jolt.

'Then six months ago, Robin was nearly killed, half stabbed to death in his garage.'

Sarah leaned forward in disbelief.

'Good God! Is he okay?'

'He *is* now, but it was touch and go.'

Alice paused for another sip of wine before continuing.

Sarah was still amazed. 'I'm surprised I never heard anything about that.'

'You wouldn't have. It was all hushed up. Robin didn't want it getting out. Would have made his life even more dangerous. It's bad enough as it is.'

'The thing is, he was *always* a bit worried about some form of retribution. You know, by people he'd put away. He'd even changed his appearance and grown a beard. And he'd gone really low profile – no Facebook or anything. Anyway, we narrowed down the people who might have done it – or ordered it to be done – to someone in jail, in Belmarsh.

'Who's *we, exactly*?' A question Sarah had to ask, even though it would irritate Alice.

'Me and Tim Marshal, Robin's son, now a Detective Sergeant. And Joe Bain, Detective Inspector at Scotland Yard, Robin's sidekick a few years ago. We went through the entire records of absolutely everyone that Robin had put away, gradually narrowing it down to the most likely one to seek revenge.'

'But surely the Hampshire police would have done that?'

'Presumably. But six months have gone by, and there doesn't seem to be any progress.'

'How frustrating.'

'And also frightening.'

Sarah put down her glass. 'How do you mean, frightening?'

'I'll tell you. I was probably stupid, but I was so incensed that someone could do that to Robin that I wangled my way into Belmarsh as a fill-in psychologist to try and find out more about our suspect. It was a catastrophe. A disaster.'

Sarah frowned. 'How? In what way?'

'First. I think I was instrumental in nearly getting a young inmate killed, probably because he talked to me about the man we suspected. And then got found out for doing that.'

'Jesus!'

'Luckily we got the boy moved. But that's not the end of it. A few weeks later – and this was all hushed up – as was the knife attack on Robin – I was driving along near Aylesbury with an old boyfriend – and we were shot at, and by a sub-machine-gun. In fact, if I hadn't driven off so fast, I wouldn't be here.'

'*Christ!*' Sarah was visibly shocked.

'And on the very same day, when they were on holiday in Spain, Robin and Pam were nearly killed by a car.'

'What? In a car crash?'

'No. By a car deliberately slamming into them when they were touring the town.'

'Good God! Are they alright?'

'Yes, but pretty shaken up as you can imagine.'

'But that could have been an accident.'

'No, they caught the people, a young English thug and a Spaniard. The Spanish police were very good, really helpful. It turned out it was another hit, definitely.'

Sarah now admitted to herself that this was indeed 'pretty big'; that is, if Alice had really got her facts right. She knew there would have to be an enormous amount of checking before she could touch the story, and not only sieving through the facts, but also consulting with her superiors whether the story could run.

'So,' Alice continued, 'we probably have an inmate in one of Her Majesty's prisons who's mad enough and determined enough to order the murder of people on the outside who he feels have caused him trouble – or could in the future. It's a horrendous situation for me and Robin. Let alone his wife and sons.'

Alice now explained more about 'Big Mack' without revealing his name, and described how he ran a huge drug business from his cell.

'I know I should be surprised, but I'm not,' admitted Sarah, shaking her head.

Alice sighed. 'Our problem is the prison service is in such a mess, what with budget cuts meaning too few staff and far too many inmates, that we don't think we can do much about it unless we put real pressure on. And that's where the media might just come in.'

Sarah thought carefully for a few moments. What Alice was putting forward was not good enough – sensational yes, but far too flimsy. But for now she decided to hear her out and leave the inevitable string of questions until later. There would certainly have to be a lot of them. But at the same time she reminded herself that Alice was no fool, putting up a brilliant defence at Ruth Isaacs' recent trial, and acting with enormous control at the trial of David Hammond three years before – and in incredibly difficult personal circumstances. She decided to give her friend some hope.

'There's no doubt that the state of the prisons is a real hot potato at the moment. In fact, at the *Mail* we've been on about it quite a lot lately – in almost something of a crusade.'

Alice nodded. 'Yes, I've noticed. In fact, that's why I'm here.'

Sarah paused. 'I don't think it would be too difficult to get my Editor to let me have a go. But I can't promise anything. We could probably run a feature, then back it up with social media. But I can't start right now. And I'll need concrete facts. Tell you what, why don't you come round on Saturday, say lunchtime? I won't have any deadlines and presumably you don't have patients then?'

'No, and I'm free all day.'

'Okay, Saturday it is. Bring any information you have – concrete information not supposition – and we'll try and work out an angle that'll *really* make people sit up. I'm still at the same address, where you came last time. But again, it's got to be hard facts rather than woolly theories. And I'd need to know a lot more about your suspect and how you narrowed it down to him. And even then, we couldn't possibly name him. Or you, come to that. The story would have to be far more general, otherwise it would be bloody difficult to give it credence.'

||||||

Sarah lived in a little flat in Adam & Eve Mews, not far from High Street Kensington, and walking distance from the Derry Street *Daily Mail* building. When Alice arrived, she noticed some sandwiches, a bottle of wine and also one of mineral water near Sarah's laptop. She thought she might stick to the water, at least for the moment. They settled down to work out how to handle the article and Sarah explained the paper's editorial position about Britain's jail situation.

'We've already been running stuff about how the prisons are getting out of control, how there aren't enough staff, with far too many prisoners and a lot of drugs. But we've never really looked at how there are *real* Czars, shadowy figures running things from *inside* the prisons – and certainly not ones who can reach outside and start threatening civilians, let alone getting them killed. But we can't name names, not unless we're a hundred per cent sure of them. And even then it would be an uphill battle.'

They worked all afternoon on the story, focussing specifically on Belmarsh, but pointing out that other prisons would almost certainly have similar situations and 'robber barons'.

Sarah tapped away, describing the fear among inmates, the terror of 'jugging' and other deterrent punishments, and even of the possibility of murders disguised as 'suicides' or 'accidents'. The article went on to detail the massive drug traffic, the lack of proper searches of either visitors or the cells and blocks, the corruption among some staff and finally the existence of masterminds like 'Big Mack', apparently untouchable by the authorities. Not to mention the all too prevalent bribes.

Finally, she printed out two copies for both of them to look at carefully. As they worked away with red pens, Sarah looked up. 'Of course, the lawyers would have to check all this out before we could run it. It's pretty explosive stuff. But I think the editors might love it – that's if it's absolutely accurate. It's really topical.'

'But do yourself a favour,' said Alice.

'What?'

'If it does come out, don't put your name to it.'

'*Why ever* not? It could raise my profile, like those articles I wrote about you.'

'Maybe. But it could be dangerous.'

'What are you saying exactly…?'

'That if he can go after me and Robin, he might want to cause trouble for someone who uses a newspaper to spoil his game.'

Sarah thought for a moment.

'Okay, I could use a pseudonym. I've done that before.'

Alice looked serious. She was suddenly beginning have second thoughts about involving her friend.

||||||

Alice's phone rang, very late and long after her last patient had left.

'Doctor Diamond? It's Alec Wilson, Thames Valley Police. Sorry to be calling so late, but something's come up that you need to know about.'

'Go ahead.'

'You know we've been on the look-out for that BMW?'

'Of course.'

'Well, we've found it. Or rather, some local kid out fishing did. There's an old quarry near Finmere, normally flooded. But with this dry weather, the level went down and revealed the roof of a car sticking out of the water.

It was dragged out, and turned out to be a BMW – so we were called in. We couldn't tell the colour, because it was completely burned out, and with the number plates removed as well. Although we *did* find the chassis number – which we've checked. Stolen months ago, in Aberdeen.'

'Do you think it's the same one that tried to ambush *me*?'

'Almost certainly. And because, I'm sorry to tell you, there were two bodies where the back seat had been. The fire hadn't left much of them, unrecognisable, melted nearly to skeletons, but forensics found their hands had been tied with wire and the skulls were almost certainly ruptured by gunshots. We're now checking dental records. In fact, the Gardai in Dublin think they may have at least one match.'

'Good God!' The description was horrific enough, even for someone with medical and police experience. But the implications were much worse.

'And the clincher was finding two cartridge cases in the back. Nine mill.'

Silence.

'Are you still there, Doctor?'

'Yes, sorry. A bit much to take in.'

'Understandably. Anyway, our immediate thought was that whoever ordered that hit on you then decided to clear up any loose ends. I know there's seldom honour among thieves, but this shows a level of vindictiveness that we've never seen before. And also, by the way, a high level of organisation.

Again, I'm really sorry to tell you all this. And I'm sure you'll have realized you're probably still in danger. I've alerted Joe Bain at the Met and the Hampshire police, and tried to call Robin Marshal, but his phone's been engaged. We'll keep you informed and be back in touch.'

Alice put the phone down. So Mack could not only try to kill people from his prison cell, he could even kill anyone who *failed* him.

Almost at once, the phone rang again. This time it was Robin Marshal. Before Alice could speak, he launched straight into his own news.

'I just had Jim Fawcett, you know my ex-police pal in Spain, on the line. About those two fellows who tried to do in me and Pam.'

'Yes, but..'

'Well, they're dead – both of them, apparently of food poisoning. But in different parts of a big prison in Malaga, served by different kitchens. Bloody suspicious, to say the least.'

'My God! But you don't surprise me.'

Robin was silent, shaken by her strange reply.

'Why? What on *earth* do you mean?'

'I was about to tell you. I've just got off the phone with Thames Valley Police. They think they've found two of those guys who tried to kill *me*. Dead, found in a quarry in a burned-out car – and probably shot.

There was silence at the end of the line. Then Robin Marshal spoke in a quiet, tired voice.

'It's all too much. I think we have to assume that Mack ordered this, though as we both know only too well, assumption's dangerous. It appears he's not only willing and able to try to knock off anyone who's crossed him, but ruthless enough to do that to his *own* people. And *still* from a prison cell. Christ! It's beyond belief. Let's meet up with Tim to talk things over.

And is there anyone *else* who should know?'

||||||

It was nearly midnight when Alice called Sarah Shaw.

'Christ Alice, it's late. What's up?'

'Where's the article?'

'They just told me. The lawyers cleared it, and they moved fast. It's coming out tomorrow, I should have told you. Isn't that great?'

Alice flinched. 'Good God! Can it be stopped?

'Stopped? Don't be silly, Alice! It's coming off the presses right now. On-line's out, and the vans with the first edition have probably left. Why? What's up? Aren't you pleased?'

Alice gave her the sinister news from both Aylesbury and Spain.

Sarah was silent, obviously shaken as she, too, hauled in the implications.

'Sarah, you know I told you to use a pseudonym?'

'Yes, and I did."

'Well, thank God for that. But if I were you, I'd still take a holiday or stay with your friends. And I'm really sorry I got you involved.'

IIIIII

When the feature appeared next day, it was huge. It was a quiet news day, so there was room to trail the article on the front page of the paper, under a bold headline, WHO RULES OUR PRISONS?

Then inside, it covered no less than four pages. There were also pictures of Belmarsh and other prisons, famous former prisoners like Ronnie Biggs and Jeffrey Archer, lines of visitors with their faces blurred and only too in-focus photographs of the Home Secretary and the ponderously named 'Lord High Chancellor Secretary of State for Justice', both of whom happened to be women.

And the impact on the Secretary of State for Justice was probably the most spectacular. Sitting behind her desk in the Ministry of Justice's offices in Petty France, she stared at the *Daily Mail* open on her desk with cold fury.

'I have to go to the House tomorrow about this. How much of this is true?'

Her Permanent Secretary cleared his throat, nervously.

'Well, all the stuff about over-crowding, under-staffing, and I suppose the drugs, is all pretty well public knowledge – although I've never seen it reported so brutally. But this is the first time these Czars or prison Napoleons have been talked about like this.'

The Justice Secretary controlled her irritation with difficulty as she stared at the group in front of her.

'What, to me, is completely unacceptable is that there are prisoners in our jails controlling a huge lucrative drug trade on their mobile phones – *illegal* phones, I might add. Visitors are arriving loaded with drugs and, partly because of some EU laws, my prison officers can't even search them properly. And it seems nobody is regularly sweeping the blocks and searching the cells for drugs or phones. And when they do, some bribed prison officer tips the inmates off, and then the stuff is moved, so they find nothing. That's if I understand things correctly.'

She paused, looking around the room. 'Is that a fair summary?'

Some of the civil servants facing her nodded glumly.

She pressed a buzzer.

'Please get the Chief Executive of NOMS on the phone.'

The civil servants glanced nervously at each other, worried that their boss was not using the 'normal channels' to reach the National Offender Management Service.

'Hello, I presume you've read the *Mail*? And I presume you don't want to be a laughing stock.

I want *you* to do something, Mr Hawkins, and do it without warning, *any* warning. You'll send in the Dedicated Search Team, what I think you call the 'ghost-busters.'

She looked up frowning, thinking she had detected a laugh in the room.

'And it needs to happen fast. Not just to catch the inmates off-guard, but frankly for political reasons.

You'll give the Governor of Belmarsh only a few hours notice of their arrival. You know how to do it well enough. Searches in groups of cells, block by block. Prisoners strip-searched in their cells. Staff outside to catch what they try to throw out. The DST will then look especially for drugs and phones, which will all be confiscated. The phones will be identified and linked to specific prisoners, who'll have their sentences reviewed. Phones to be analysed by another specialist electronics team. Police will then quickly be visiting any of the people the inmates have been calling.

That same day, visitors will then be let in, the doors locked behind them and then told that for special reasons the normal rules won't apply that day. They'll then be searched much more carefully than usual. If they're found to be smuggling drugs or phones, they'll be arrested and taken straight round to Woolwich Police Station and charged, with evidence of outside collusion gathered. They'll then be held on remand.

Any visitors who are clean will be let go and told they can come back tomorrow. Stress that the Belmarsh staff must be *extremely* polite throughout. The last thing we want to do is give lawyers extra ammunition, or visiting families for that matter. And all we can do is to handle the media as best we can. We need them on our side as much as they need us on theirs. All of them will now be on the *Mail's* bandwagon. And all media calls *must* be referred to our Press Office.

Is all that clear, Mr Hawkins? Good. Some of my people from here will visit Belmarsh later today. I'll be in touch. Goodbye.'

She looked up with a strong hint of defiance at her amazed group of civil servants. She had a much better grasp of prison procedures than they could ever have imagined.

'I'm not worried about budgets or the money for this. I'll find it.' She pointed to the *Daily Mail* on the table. 'But I'm *not* going to tolerate anything like this again.'

She closed the file in front of her.

' And I want all the relevant department heads back here at two. No later. It's time to get on with it. And *fast.*'

CHAPTER 24

BELMARSH PRISON

Apart from the Ministry of Justice and the House of Commons, there was, of course, another place where the *Daily Mail* feature caused a considerable stir. And that was in Her Majesty's Prison, Belmarsh.

It hadn't been much fun for the Governor, getting that call from NOMS under pressure from the Justice Secretary – roasting him. *It wasn't fair*, he smarted. *With all the budget cuts, he simply couldn't control things – especially the drugs – as he might have wished.*

He passed on his displeasure to his senior officers at that morning's staff meeting, so everyone was soon on edge. But he could *not* tell anyone yet about the DST raid.

And then, to call Big Mack 'on edge', would have been the understatement of the year. Most cons favoured *The SUN*, but it wouldn't take long for someone, suppressing a smirk, to bring him the *Daily Mail* – which they did the same day.

He read through the whole article with mounting fury and concern. He could see the danger at once. The article had not named him, but anyone in Belmarsh would know exactly whom it was talking about. And although it was apparently written by a 'Lucinda Cox', he could guess exactly who had fixed all this.

That bitch, the shrink. I'd bloody tried to eliminate her, but nothing seems to have worked. Whatever I do next better work, but everything will be much harder to fix if we lose phones.

'FUCK THE BITCH!' Mack screamed to his cronies, his face contorted with anger. 'It must have been her who talked to the bloody paper. And why don't we do in the reporter, too? Except we don't know who she is. My people say there's no Lucinda Cox with the paper, or even attached to it. So, a false fucking name. And why don't we do in the paper for that matter, while we're at it?'

After quite a while, with nobody daring to interrupt his ranting fury, he calmed down a little.

'Bill, when's your sister next in?'

'Should be tomorrow, Mack. Although she was pretty shaken up by the random search during that raid during her last visit. Luckily, for once she had nothing on her.'

'Well, make damned sure she gets the notes I'll give her, and then passes them on, and quickly.'

He had another thought.

'And where's that Arab fellow who just got out of HSU? Tell him I want to talk to him during Association.'

CHAPTER 25

HASLEMERE

Alice was standing on John's bathroom scales, worried to see that she had lost another two pounds. Only seven stone ten. Just last night John had run his finger down her spine, remarking that she was 'skin and bone'. And she was afraid her dramatic loss of weight was beginning to affect their sex-life, which until quite recently had been better than it ever was. John had now told her several times that he was almost becoming afraid of crushing her in bed. And she had told him, on just as many occasions since the shooting incident, that she wasn't in the mood, though at least he understood why.

When they had first met over three years ago, sex with John had been more comfortable than exciting, and had somehow missed a certain buzz – a major reason, she now fully recognized, why she had been so powerfully attracted to the enigmatic David Hammond. It would be a terrible shame, she thought, if worry and weight-loss now threatened her new relationship with John.

And today would be an even bigger hurdle. At lunch-time she would have to see his parents again, and if she remembered Astri, force down a gargantuan meal. Not to mention an incredibly embarrassing one, during which the conversation would surely be unbearably stilted and awkward. For the umpteenth time she wondered whether she should duck out of it, but knew how bitterly disappointed John would be, and that if she refused to go, it might become, and almost certainly would – a major problem between them. She had no choice but to agree, dreading it though she was.

Getting dressed, she pictured the strain of it all yet again. It would be anything but easy for any of them. It had to be exceptionally rare for parents to entertain a son's girlfriend knowing she had cheated on him with someone who'd turned out to be a serial killer, even if it were three years ago. All of it would still be totally fresh in their minds. The lurid newspaper headlines. The photos of her and Hammond. The journalists at their doors. The neighbours' shocked or smirking faces. The TV coverage of the court case. And then the news of Hammond's death after an attack in prison, which had opened up the story all over again.

How could John do this to her? But what she couldn't do to *him* was refuse to go. An only son, he was deeply close to them, as they were in return. And if their own relationship were going to have any chance of working, she had no choice.

John was pleased to see her come downstairs in the violet dress he liked, and with the brooch he had given her years ago.

'You look great!' He smiled to see the brooch, and Alice not in her usual trousers, but a pretty dress.

'Thanks.'

He looked at his watch – just after twelve.

'Fancy a drink before we go?'

Alice certainly did. And a stiff one. 'I wouldn't mind a gin and tonic.'

A quarter of an hour later, they set off for Haslemere, and for another fifteen minutes neither of them spoke.

John patted her on her lap. 'It'll be alright. Don't worry, trust me.'

Another long silence as Alice pictured his parents, and the house and garden she remembered so well – Arthur's study – full of equipment to explore mosses in his profession as a leading bryologist, the kitchen, equally full of his mother's flower paintings – and the beautiful garden beyond.

'Have a cigarette if you want,' said John, realising how tense she was. 'I don't mind, as long as you open the window.'

He normally *did* mind, and she had almost given up, but today she had a pack of ten in her bag and probably craved for one – understandably.

'Remember, Alice, not a word about what happened in Buckingham, or the quarry, or Spain. And if the subject of that exposé in the *Daily Mail* comes up, get off it as soon as possible – or say you haven't read it.' Alice didn't need reminding – *again*.

All too soon for her, John was parking his Morgan in his parents' drive and his father was coming out to greet them, with Astri presumably preparing one of her usual gargantuan meals in the kitchen.

||||||

'Thanks, Astri, that went really well. Must have been a heck of a strain for her.'

Astri flinched. 'And us.'

'I know, but we did the right thing.'

'But I can't help thinking wondering if *John* is. Can you *really* go back after all that, pretend that nothing ever happened and wipe the slate clean?'

Arthur hesitated. I don't know. But that's up to him to decide, not us. We've still got a son, that's the important bit.'

He looked at the mess on the kitchen table.

'Let's leave all this and go and have a rest.'

||||||

'Well, that wasn't too bad, was it?' said John in the car a minute or two after they'd left, and rather too breezily and ebulliently for Alice.

'Better than I thought it would be. But frankly, not easy. Quite a few sticky moments and places we couldn't go.'

'But they *did* seem pleased to see you.'

'John, don't be silly. They *had* to seem pleased, even if they weren't. That's just good manners. They could hardly have looked at me with horror for the whole meal. For God's sake, they were doing the whole thing for *you*.'

'Darling, you're such a pessimist.'

'No, just a realist.'

Silence fell for a while.

'But your Mum *was* nice to talk about my *Psychology Today* article – and even have it open on the right page on the sofa. A sort of nod in my direction. And it *was* a delicious lunch.'

'Good to see you eat,' added John. 'About time, too.'

He thought for a bit.

'What did Mum say to you when you were out in the garden?'

'Not much. Asked a bit about my work. Talked a bit about how so many people were struggling with things today, and whether I found it uphill running a psychology practice. Chatted a bit about your father, too – and your sister. Your Mum's obviously finding it a wee bit difficult to adjust to your sister and her girlfriend getting married and adopting a child. But she did say one nice thing that really surprised me.'

'What?'

'That she knew I must have been through hell.'

John patted her on the knee. 'Well, that's a step in the right direction!'

'John, it's not that simple. If we stay an item, and I seriously hope we do, there'll always be a shadow – on both sides. That's inevitable. Time heals some things, but it doesn't eradicate memories easily. You're old enough to know that, and also to know that certain things will never be forgotten.'

'But forgiven is a good start.'

John paused, deciding to change the subject. 'For me, the biggest relief of lunch was when you pretended you hadn't read the *Daily Mail*, and so had no idea about the prison exposé she banged on about.'

'I could hardly admit I was involved. And frankly, I thought it was pretty tactless of her to bring the subject up at all.'

'Why?'

'She must have known that any mention of prisons would immediately remind me of David Hammond.'

'Alice, don't be too harsh on her, and if you don't want to be reminded of prisons, why did you work in Belmarsh?'

'You know why. I was trying to help Robin.'

A silence fell in the car.

'Alice, what *really* worries me is what happens when the news of your attempted murder gets out, in fact, your *double* attempted murder. Frankly, I'm amazed it's been kept under wraps so far. And why it has. If it ever gets out, it would make Mum and Dad freak out completely.'

Ten minutes passed in silence and they were now approaching Guildford, where Alice was again reminded of David Hammond and that blaring opera music he played when driving past it with her.

'Mind if I have another cigarette?'

'Suppose not. If you really must.'

'One on the way there for courage, and this one for relief.'

'Do you want to go out tonight?' asked John a mile or two later.

'Good God, no. At least, not for a meal. I've eaten enough for three.'

'No, just for a glass of champagne.'

Alice laughed. 'Champagne, why? What are we celebrating?'

'The fact we've broken the ice.'

Alice fell into silence, suddenly envisaging a vast ice-covered lake, in which much of the ice would never be broken. Constant perma-frost.

John knew exactly the way she was thinking. 'Darling, you're such a bloody pessimist,' he repeated, but this time laughing.

Alice's phone suddenly buzzed with a text. It was Mary Bloomfield from Belmarsh.

SEARCH RAID TOMORROW. M.

CHAPTER 26

BELMARSH PRISON

There was no warning of the search – just as the Justice Secretary had demanded.

Two days later, the normal announcement of 'ASSOCIATION ' did not come over the loudspeakers, and the prisoners wondered why they were not filing out into the exercise yard as they did every day.

Even less normal was the sudden clatter of boots in the blocks as dozens of unfamiliar officers poured in. Experienced inmates immediately guessed what was up. It was the Dedicated Search Team, the 'ghost-busters' that nobody had seen in months. And it became quickly obvious that they were there to search the whole prison, not just selected blocks.

'Big Mack' was one of the first to become worried by this unexpected turn of events. Through the window in his cell door he whispered to one of the warders, 'Why didn't you fuckin' tell us?'

'We had no idea, mate, not until a few minutes ago. We're as surprised as you are. Anyway, better not be seen talking to me.' He moved away.

Jesus, I pay these bastards enough, and then they still know nothing! And I bet it's that shrink bitch who's caused this fuck-up. This time she gets it, and no more mistakes.

The prisoners locked in their cells could tell exactly what was happening. The DST teams were coming down the block, searching five cells at a time. Faced by what was obviously a very thorough search indeed, there were many inmates who realised that this was no ordinary raid – it was something special, and for anyone who had anything stashed away, a very dangerous situation. Several went to the windows and threw things out – drugs and phones – dismayed to see that prison officers were instantly retrieving them and carefully noting the cell positions from which they had come.

When it was Big Mack's turn, he was fairly confident – not stupid enough to keep anything like phones in his own cell. Some nearby inmate could take the rap. Nor was he fazed by having to be strip-searched. By now, he was used to it.

The DST people could shortly be heard wheeling trolleys along the walkways of the blocks, obviously loaded with evidence, and the prisoners in cells yet to be searched knew exactly what they were after – drugs and the phones with which to order them. And they also knew that any prisoners found with either would almost certainly have their sentences reviewed or increased. But nobody was going to cause any trouble. They knew all too well that a Tornado team might be there, out of sight, just waiting to pounce.

As he stood half-naked in the centre of his cell, 'Big Mack' had become deeply disturbed. His mobile phones were absolutely vital to him, not just for the running of his empire, but to nail that shrink bitch.

Several inmates were found to have phones and told they would be attending punishment parade, or 'Nickings', in the morning, and Mack knew soon enough that the DST had nailed him. The hiding place for his phones was in the very next cell and its occupant whispered the bad news that it had been found. While he would willingly take the rap, a few days of examination of the phone might reveal the real user and his contacts on the outside.

Until we can get some phones back in here, we'll be back to passing notes through the visitor system – wives and girlfriends. Uselessly slow and out of control.

It took until four in the afternoon for the raid to be over. Many prisoners had been served notices about attending 'nickings' in the morning. They were furious. First, with the Governor and his staff. It was irrational, of course. After all, the prison should have been running like this anyway. Only the Government's budget cuts, the lack of staff and the sense of defeatism had let the situation get so far in the prisoners' favour.

But 'Big Mack' was intelligent enough to realize that resentment could quickly build against *him*. After all, he and his companions had assured everyone that they had everything under control; the warders fixed, the prisoners quiet, the visitors obeying orders. Now things appeared to have changed. Trouble had started. Why? Everyone was beginning to suffer. What had prompted this? Mack knew he'd have to do something to retrieve the situation. But *what*?

It didn't help to hear more bad news the next day. While the big search was taking place, many of the visitors – the wives, girlfriends and partners – had also been searched and many arrested. The place was beginning to resemble a proper prison.

And all because of that bloody cow.

||||||

The next day, after 'Association', several members of Mack's closest team came to his cell. It was Bill Jessop who first addressed him.

'Mack, we need to talk.'

'What the fuck about?' he responded belligerently, although he knew exactly what it was likely to be about.

'Everything's screwed up, Mack, and you know why.'

'No, I *don't* know why. Why don't you fucking *tell* me.'

Bill was nearly as big as Mack and just as prone to violence, and was not going to be intimidated by bluster. Not this time.

'Ever since you decided to go for people on the outside, people you wanted to get revenge on, there's been trouble. You know we've got a nice little number going here – lots of money for our retirement. Secret bank accounts and so on. But it all needed to be hidden, without rocking the boat. But what we've got *now* is newspapers on to us, no phones to get things going, and any amount of pissed-off cons. It's a bloody disaster.'

While furious that his authority was being questioned, in a way Mack knew that Bill was right. He'd been breaking too many key rules. Perhaps time for a pause?

'Okay, okay! I'll cool it. And then we can try and get things moving again.'

When they'd gone, he suddenly remembered that without a phone there was no quick method of stopping or changing anything imminently, and no way of recalling anyone, or aborting a mission, or indeed of controlling events.

The raid and search, far from preventing him from starting things, had actually prevented him from *stopping* them.

And now there could be *real* trouble.

CHAPTER 27

PUTNEY

Alice picked up her ringing phone.

'Was that you, Alice, behind that article in the *Mail?*' It was Robin Marshal, not sounding at all happy.

'How do you mean?'

'You know – the story, and then the raid.'

Alice hesitated, regretting she hadn't consulted him. 'Partly, but not the raid.'

'But they were bound to do a raid after an exposure like that. I wish you'd told us before you did it.'

'Well, we seemed to be getting nowhere, so I thought I could put on a bit of pressure. And I also thought…'

Robin interrupted. 'I can see what you thought, but you're not the police. And unless they move the bastard, he'll soon be back controlling things. And, more important, he's going to be *really* pissed off about what you've done. That's if he thinks you were involved as he almost certainly will.'

Alice was chastened but still positive. 'Surely he wouldn't try anything new?'

'Why not? We've all agreed he might try anything.'

'Oh, God.'

She heard Robin sigh.

'Look, let's try to meet early next week– and in the meantime, watch your back for God's sake. And call me or Tim if you see anything suspicious.'

Alice had scarcely put the phone down, when it rang again. This time it was John.

'I've just re-read that article. And I have to say, I'm bloody worried.'

Alice sighed. *Not another lecture.*

'Has anything happened, Alice, you know as a result?'

'Well, there was a huge raid. They took away lots of drugs and mobile phones. And at least, for a while, he may not be able to start anything. Big Mack, I mean.'

There was a pause.

'Yes, but he may not be able to *stop* things, either.'

Another silence.

'Look, I really think you shouldn't be alone in that big old Putney house. I know the police are meant to drive by several times a day, but I don't call that *real* protection. I really think you ought to move in with me. At least, until this is resolved. And hopefully, longer.'

'I'm beginning to think the same way myself.'

'About time! Then let's agree that we'll move more of your stuff this weekend.'

'Okay.'

'The only trouble is that tomorrow I have to be up north, as I said, for a really early morning meeting in Manchester. Will you be okay tonight?'

'Sure. Don't forget I've got a gun.'

'Alice, for God's sake, I don't want any mention of guns. Take this seriously. Just lock up properly and keep the alarm system on all night – may be a nuisance, but it's worth it.'

||||||

That evening, Alice did exactly as she was told – but unusually –

sat down at her dressing table before going early to bed, noticing that she somehow looked stressed, older, and not surprisingly.

The last few months had clearly taken their toll, and as John had suggested, she should rethink her life and take things easier. Forget about work – at least, outside working hours – worry less about other people, make more time for hobbies, read a bit more – and not psychology tomes – simply chill out and enjoy herself a bit more. But how could she in the circumstances? And if she couldn't, how could she ever help other people, let alone herself? She suddenly felt afraid. And a fraud.

She knew, frighteningly, she was becoming an island to which others were finding it ever harder to reach, too immersed in her own problems to listen properly to those of other people. And what kind of qualification was that for someone in her profession? Disastrous!

Suddenly, she was startled by a loud bang outside. She went nervously to the curtains and looked out of the window. The normally empty and dark Common had filled up with people, adults and children.

A rocket arched into the sky and exploded.

She had quite forgotten it was Guy Fawkes Night.

CHAPTER 28

PUTNEY, LONDON

Why do firework displays have to go on so late?

Lying in her pyjamas, Alice was fuming, although telling herself not to be a killjoy. But surely fireworks were mostly for children, who should be going to bed by now? She loved children, but suddenly it was all too much.

Outside on Putney Common, and right opposite her house, there was a huge bonfire celebrating Guy Fawkes night, and round it a crowd watching a firework display. It was now after eleven, and Alice had to get up really early the next morning. It was getting irritating. Even with the curtains drawn, the flashes of light came into her bedroom, and the noise was loud and continuous – so there was no chance of sleep.

The house wasn't normally noisy. In fact it was often *too* quiet. Ever since she had inherited it from her father, Alice had wondered if it really suited her. It was, after all, pretty big and she found she really only used her bedroom and the kitchen – and her consulting room, of course. And the garden? When was she last out there?

It was also too cluttered and a bit gloomy too, with all the furniture that she'd never got around to sorting and a lovely old grandfather clock she'd never even wound up. But tonight there was no problem of too much silence.

Then suddenly she heard a new noise, and a very different one. A crash, downstairs.

Something or someone had clearly smashed in her front door. *And why hadn't the alarm gone off?* Alice crept in her pyjamas to her bedroom door, her heart pounding. All the warnings from Robin and John that she was still in danger came flooding back.

Why the hell had she stayed here?

She looked down. The front door was wide open, with the hall lit by the fireworks. And there was definitely someone down there – and someone strong enough to smash his way in.

She closed her bedroom door and locked it as slowly and quietly as she could. *That won't stop him for long.*

Her mind flashed back to the past – and a bearded figure three years ago – coming slowly up the stairs to kill her.

Right now she might be just as terrified, but at least she was no longer defenceless.

She fumbled in her handbag for her keys – hugely relieved that she had, unusually, taken it upstairs, not leaving it in the kitchen, and went over and opened her main dress cupboard. There in the corner, in the dim light, was the tall grey regulation armoured gun case. As quickly as she could, she turned the key in the top lock, and then the lower one, opened the door and felt for her Spanish AYA twenty-bore.

On top of the gun case were two cartridges. Some instinct, probably based on Hammond's attack three years ago, had made her keep them there. She took out the gun, broke it open and inserted the cartridges with a soft 'clunk'.

Alice now crept round her bed, and knelt down with her back to the window, the room still sporadically illuminated by the firework flashes. The barrel of the shotgun stretched out towards the door, and she felt her hands shaking, forcing her to tighten her grip.

She slid forward the safety catch.

Suddenly the door burst open, and a large figure in heavy

clothing was lit up by the fireworks, steadying himself from the effort of kicking open the door, with a glint of metal from a weapon – still pointing downwards.

Alice didn't hesitate. She aimed at the man's lower body and fired the top barrel and then the choke, the flashes almost blinding her.

There was a scream of agony and the figure staggered backwards – in a clatter of shots.

Christ, he's got a machine-gun, and I've fired my only cartridges!

But the doorway was empty. The man had gone, lurching down the stairs.

Alice waited a few tense moments, then reached for her mobile with a shaking hand, barely able to dial 999.

||||||

A police car, blue lights flashing, had forced its way through the firework crowds. It wasn't the usual one from Wandsworth police station that was meant to be checking on her house. It was a BMW, with three Armed Response Officers with flak jackets and Heckler & Koch sub-machine guns. But they had nothing to respond to, at least with firearms, because Alice's assailant had gone, although he had certainly left his mark.

With the lights turned on, she looked down. It was obvious that he had been very badly hurt, with a trail of blood across the beige carpet, and all down the stairs. And according to the shouts of the police, out into the garden. A huge effort for him to escape.

Alice had left her shotgun on the bed. 'I haven't ejected the spent cartridges,' she told the first policeman who'd arrived, a Sergeant. 'And my shotgun certificate's downstairs if you need it.' Walking down the stairs, now in a dressing-gown, she was clearly very shaken and the Sergeant helped her into a chair in the kitchen.

Another policeman, uniformed, suddenly burst in, sweating and breathing heavily. He'd obviously been running. He stared around him.

'Christ. What happened?'

'She got attacked,' said the Armed Response Sergeant, rather coldly. 'And who are you?'

'Derek Shaw, from Wandsworth. We're meant to come by here every half an hour or so, but we got blocked by a woman picking up kids from the fireworks and jamming her car across Egliston Road. We had to go right round and stop by the church – nearly a mile. I saw the blue lights and started running.'

As soon as he'd left, talking into his radio, the whole house except the kitchen was blocked off, and the forensics team in their white clothing got to work. The doors and bannisters were checked for fingerprints, as were the cartridge cases littering the landing. Two dog teams had gone out into the street and then on to the Common – although the milling crowds of people and the strong smell of fireworks probably made their tracking job difficult or even impossible. In the kitchen, Alice busied herself giving out cups of tea, wishing she could drink something stronger.

The Sergeant could not disguise his admiration.

'You must have hit him hard, Miss. And somewhere pretty vulnerable.'

'Well, I noticed his heavy clothing, like a donkey jacket. I thought light Number Seven pellets from a twenty bore might not have got through, so I went for him a bit lower.'

The Sergeant flinched, imagining where, astonished by Alice's composure and apparent knowledge of firearms.

'Ouch!' The remark came from a new figure, in plain clothes, who'd just joined them and flashed his warrant card at the Sergeant. Alice was hugely relieved to see it was Tim Marshal. He smiled at her reassuringly, before turning to the Sergeant.

'I know Dr Diamond, and I also know something about what might be going on. Can I have a word with her, and then you?'

Tim then took Alice to one side, shaking his head.

'Heard it from my colleagues and luckily wasn't far away. Well, now you can *really* see why Dad and I were so worried.'

Alice nodded, 'Yes, I know. I was far too over-confident. And stupid. I'm really sorry.'

Just then, one of the forensics team leaned into the kitchen. 'We've found eight empty nine mill cases, and holes in the carpet. He must have involuntarily squeezed the trigger when he was hit – with the gun, probably an UZI – pointing downwards. And it looks as if he may have also shot himself in the foot – quite literally.'

While one or two officers smiled at the pun, this time such gallows humour was lost on Alice, who could see nothing funny in the situation. Nothing appeared to be able to stop that evil man in Belmarsh. *If it were that man,* she reminded herself.

The Sergeant said, more seriously, 'And if he *did* hit his foot, he wouldn't have made it very far, especially if *you* got him in the groin as well. Ouch!'

||||||

But he *had* made it, at least as far as the escape car parked round the corner in Egliston Road. He opened the door and slumped into the passenger seat groaning with pain, throwing the sub-machine gun to the floor.

The driver noted the blood pouring on to the upholstery, and with clear irritation.

'What the hell happened?'

'She fockin' shot *me*! She had a gun.'

'But did you get *her*?' There was little sympathy.

'No, she got me *first*. And in the fockin' balls! *Get me to a hospital.* No, a doctor, *fast*! He gasped with pain. 'Christ, this is *agony*.'

'Sure, mate. No worries. Now, crouch down, and keep right out of sight.'

With its moaning passenger, the black Range-Rover with its tinted windows pulled away from the curb, nosing at first slowly through the crowds coming away from the fireworks display and then, freed from them, speeding up over the railway bridge by the Putney Leisure Centre, pausing to let a police Volvo, lights and siren on, roar past.

After crossing the Upper Richmond Road, the driver turned up a deserted tree-lined street. And outside a darkened house, he suddenly slowed, pulled over and stopped, but kept the engine running.

'Why are you stopping? Is this the doc...'

'Keep down!'

His passenger leaned forward.

Thunk.

The driver had used his silenced 9mm Glock 23 to shoot his passenger in the side of the head, and while he was conveniently slumped down.

Good. The window was untouched, with nothing to see from outside.

He put the car back into drive, pulled out and headed west.

Another body for the woods. More blood and brains all over my car.

And even more to explain to Mack.

CHAPTER 29

CHESSINGTON

It was a lovely crisp November morning in the woods and Holly and Hugo were fifty yards ahead of their parents, looking for 'Mattie', their retriever, who had suddenly disappeared.

The family came here for a walk nearly every Sunday morning – pleasantly easy to get to, just one exit away off the M25 motorway that encircled London, and also conveniently close to the 'Chessington World of Adventures', another place the kids loved.

'Daddy, Daddy! Mattie's found something, and she won't stop digging!'

Ben and Belinda Johnson strolled up the path that divided the wood from the golf course in no hurry to see what the dog was after – probably the remains of someone's picnic. But like many ten-year-olds, Holly could be very impatient, and decided she couldn't wait for them. She plunged into the dell, fifty feet further down.

'MATTIE, WHAT ARE YOU DOING?' they heard her shout.

And then there was a scream.

Her father didn't hesitate, rushing in to where the scream had come from, stumbling down the bank and disappearing. Hugo clutched his mother's hand as they heard him shout, 'MATTIE, GET OFF!'

Then, getting closer, gently talking to Holly. ' Don't cry, darling. Now, let's take the dog and go to Mummy. LEAVE IT, MATTIE!'

Ben brought Holly out of the bushes, tears streaming down her face. The dog was now on its lead, plainly still very over-excited. Belinda rushed to cuddle her daughter, while little Hugo looked on confused and frightened.

Ben squatted down and hugged Holly.

'Darling, why don't you be very grown-up and take Hugo and Mattie over to that bench there? Mummy and I need to talk. Keep her on the lead. Okay? Good girl.'

When they were out of earshot, Ben took out his phone. Before dialling, he whispered to Belinda, 'There's a body in there. All smashed up. Badly hidden. I'd say the foxes have been at it. I'll phone the police.' He just had enough signal.

'Police, please.' A pause.

'My name's Ben Johnson. I'm with my family, walking our dog. And we've just found a dead body.'

He had plainly been asked where he was, and raised his head to look around.

'On the path skirting Chessington Wood, about six hundred yards from the car park on the A 243. Actually, I can see we're just by the twelfth green of the golf course.' A pause. 'Yes, of *course* we'll stay here.'

Within a commendably short time, a police Land-Rover was bumping along from the main road. It stopped on the path and a uniformed Sergeant and a constable got out. Ben showed them where to look, and it didn't take long for them to emerge and start using a radio. Soon, another Land-Rover – a long wheelbase one – turned up and officers went into the wood with what looked like a collapsible tent. Next to arrive was a van, with two men and a woman who quickly dressed-up in white suits – and finally a sniffer dog team.

The Johnsons, or at least Ben and Holly, gave statements, with Holly, now largely recovered and rather proud of herself. And then they were told they could go home.

But just before they set off, there was a loud shout from one of the dog team about a hundred yards further on.

'SERGEANT, OVER HERE! THERE'S ANOTHER ONE!'

IIIIII

Alice happened to be visiting Robin Marshal when the call came in to him from Joe Bain at Scotland Yard. Robin explained that Alice was with him, before putting it on loudspeaker.

'Something's come up. Actually, two things. A family and their dog have just found a body in a wood near Chessington. From the initial forensics, we're pretty sure it's the fellow who came to your house and tried to kill you. He'd been badly wounded in the groin area, by shot-gun pellets – and also multiple times in the right foot by another firearm.'

'Sounds right,' responded Alice, remembering the clatter of the sub-machinegun.

'But *that's* not what killed him. He was shot in the head at close range, probably by a pistol.'

Alice was astounded, as was Robin who interjected, 'Good Lord, Joe. Certainly looks as if someone wanted him out of the way. Someone with no time for a failed, wounded man. And that would be the right direction for a vehicle leaving Putney by the A3.'

'That's what my chaps figured. We'll be matching the blood found inside Alice's house and outside on the pavement, and we'll be seeing if fingerprints reveal a suspect – or should I say victim?' Joe paused on the other end of the line.

'But that's not all. The police dogs then scoured the rest of the woods to see if there were any more clues. And what they found was *another* body.'

'Good God!' Alice literally gasped.

'And one that's been there for much longer, so not in great condition. And the foxes have been at it. He'd been shot in the back of the head, execution-style. No further ballistic evidence so far. But we *did* lift fingerprints. And you'd be amazed. Remember that prison officer whom I'm not meant to know about? The one at Belmarsh who betrayed you, Alice, and nearly let the Campbell kid get killed? Principal Officer Phillips, wasn't that his name?'

'Yup,' Alice nodded. *How could she forget?*

'Well, it's him. God knows why they killed him. Maybe he got greedy or something and asked for more money. Anyway, the police aren't finished. They're still digging around. Someone may be making a habit of dumping bodies in that wood.

Anyway, I've got to go. Just been summoned upstairs for a meeting with the boss. Remember those meetings, Robin? I'll bet you're bloody pleased not to have them any more. I'll be in touch. Bye.' Click.

Alice and Robin stared at each other.

'This is going from bad to worse,' sighed Robin. 'It finally confirms, or pretty well confirms, that we've got the right man. And it also shows he's completely ruthless and more than a little mad. Seemingly prepared to order the elimination of anyone who crosses him or fails him, or now it appears, even *inconveniences* him.'

Alice shuddered. Where had she encountered *that* kind of man before?

'It's like Stalin and the 1923 Politburo,' said Robin.

Alice was puzzled, not knowing what on earth he was talking about.

'Sorry, Alice. I keep forgetting you share few of my strange interests. Well,' he relented, '*some* of my interests. Stalin, in his paranoia, had, by the mid-thirties, killed off *all* his old friends and colleagues in the Soviet government, the 1923 Politburo.' He smiled. 'Stalin made Hitler look like a really nice, loyal, friendly, collegial pal.'

He got to his feet and went to pour them both a drink, looking back at her over his shoulder, 'I think we'd better call Tim, don't you? And a few other people.'

He came back with the drinks. 'And, by the way, however clever Big Mack may be *himself*, he's certainly not very well served by others, is he? We've *both* been saved by sloppiness and blunders, thank God. And, just imagine the stupidity of having *two* bodies dumped in the same wood? Complete madness!'

CHAPTER 30

KENSINGTON

Alice suddenly remembered someone else at potential risk. She tapped in the now familiar mobile number.

'Sarah Shaw.'

'Hi, it's me.'

'Hi. Well, that certainly stirred things up a bit, didn't it? You've probably heard the Home Secretary went ballistic, and they've started searches all over the place. And especially at Belmarsh. It's really got people talking. And circulation's shot up. Pity I didn't use my name!'

'No, Sarah – it's *not*. Thank God you *didn't*. In fact you're probably in real danger, even using a pseudonym.'

There was a sudden silence. 'Danger? Why? What do you mean?

'I've just been attacked *again*. And here in my own home.'

'Christ! Are you okay?'

'Yes, just about. You remember I mentioned taking up shooting?'

'Yes.'

'Well, I managed to get him with the shotgun I use for clays. I had only two cartridges, but I got him, wounded him. And then he literally shot himself in the foot with a sub-machine-gun.'

There was a shocked pause.

'Christ! I don't *believe* what I'm hearing! You shot someone?'

'Yes, and it gets worse. The same man I hit was found a couple of days later – in a wood. Shot in the head. And then nearby they found the body of that prison officer I think I mentioned. Also shot in the head.'

Another silence at the other end.

'Sarah, listen, the guy who's ordering this is clearly both murderous *and* mad. He really does his homework and makes sure he finds things out – like about people's houses, flats and cars, and their movements. So I'm not sure how effective a pseudonym like 'Lucinda Cox' may be, or for how long. I'm *really* sorry I got you involved in all this.'

There was another protracted silence before Sarah came back, thankfully sounding quite calm.

'Bloody hell. Sounds as if you're right. Maybe I ought to go and camp out with a friend for a while. And I'll tell my bosses here about this. They were confident enough about getting into this, but none of us could ever imagine it going *this* far. They'll alert security about the building, and anyone trying to get in. Shit, what a mess.'

||||||

Ahmed was very puzzled. He'd had his initial instructions – and then not a word. But he had enough to go ahead and make his preparations.

Of course they'd need a vehicle, inconspicuous – the kind you'd see often in that street. He first thought of one that looked as if it belonged to the actual newspaper, but there weren't very many of them, and security might be familiar with them. A delivery van? White or black, perhaps. Then, he had thought, much better would be a Royal Mail one. He'd read there were no less than 35,000 of them, familiar on pretty well every street. And Royal Mail would regularly be selling off the old ones – removing the decal stripes, the logotypes and numbers – but leaving the red paint.

It took only four days to find one at auction for less than £500. A paint shop friend then got new Royal Mail decals and tidied things up, and soon he had quite a smart red Ford Transit, looking fairly new and respectable. The expired MOT, and no road tax or insurance were of no concern to him.

He wondered why the Brothers wanted to hit a newspaper. Ahmed didn't read the English papers and had no idea what this one had been going on about. Something to do with Syria or Libya? Contempt for Da'eesh or Al Quaeda? Lack of respect for Muslims? Insulting Allah or the Prophet? Again, it was of no concern to him. He was sure the Brothers must have a good reason for such a high-profile attack. But for him it only meant money. The less questions asked, the better.

In a lock-up garage in Surbiton, they began loading the explosives into the van. The two bigger men had the heavy job of lifting the bags of jagged metal pieces to pack round the bags of the fertilizer explosives – to increase the shrapnel effect. The wiring – done by their electronics expert, Ali, peering though his glasses – had to be especially carefully prepared, slowly and methodically. Similarly, the radio detonator. Because this was to be no suicide bomb. It was to be driven to the objective and left parked outside, with the device detonated safely by radio pulses from about two hundred metres away – just like the now notorious 'Improvised Explosive Devices', or IEDs, in the Middle East.

Ahmed reckoned it would be fairly easy. He had checked out the street and the building itself. There seemed to be no really serious security, no blocking concrete barriers like those in front of the Houses of Parliament, no gates like Downing Street, and no armed roadblocks as in Baghdad or Pakistan. You could say a 'soft target', he thought.

He waited for the word. The money had arrived, big money – so all was ready.

However, he still wondered who cared enough about a newspaper to attack it.

CHAPTER 31

WANDSWORTH, LONDON

'My Mummy and Daddy are getting us a puppy for Christmas. A poodle, not like Grandad's Benny. He's very sweet, but a bit big. They found him in a dogs' home.'

'Lucky you. We're not allowed pets. At least not a dog.'

'Why not?'

'Mummy's got asthma. She's allergic to dogs.'

'Well, that's alright. You can come and play with him at our house.'

Julie Marshal was five and chatting to her little friend Melody. Satchels on their backs, they were walking in front of their mothers, with a long stream of other parents, some holding their children's hands, others clutching scooters.

The school gates were only yards away when an Audi suddenly came alongside Julie. Nobody gave it a second glance, assuming it was more parents dropping off another kid.

But then one of its back doors suddenly flew open and Julie walked straight into it, and a man jumped out and tried to drag her inside.

Sophie Marshal didn't hesitate. Years of police and karate training immediately kicked in as she felled him to the ground. Her daughter backed screaming into the crowd.

The furious onlookers surged forward and the man, confused, looked around in panic and then scrambled back into the car. The driver tried to drive off, but just then a big van delivering school supplies stopped and blocked the road in front of it. A mother's Volvo 4 X 4 was right behind, so now the Audi could not move either way.

The crowd now surrounded it, banging furiously on its roof and windows. Some were phoning – almost certainly calling the police.

Suddenly the occupants opened the doors and leapt out.

Now the screaming reached a new pitch, as the driver, wearing a balaclava, had a gun – and was waving it around at the crowd.

There was a stricken few seconds before he shouted something to his mate and they both ran off past the delivery van and out into the main street.

The trapped Audi now sat there with its doors open, and with its engine running until a man helpfully leaned in and turned the ignition off, immediately wondering if he should have done that – probably obscuring fingerprints.

Julie clung to her mother, screaming, as the first police car turned up.

||||||

'Mrs Marshal, is this your daughter?' Sitting in the Headmistress's study, the policewoman leaned forward and showed Sophie a colour photograph.

Sophie looked at it. 'Yes, that's Julie.'

'And can you think where it was taken?'

That was all too easy. She could see their blue front door and even its number. 'God. It's *our* house. Where did you find this?'

'On the passenger seat of the car. That's how they must have known which kid to snatch. They'd have followed you in the past as well, to find the school.'

So someone had been stalking the family? Sophie shuddered, trying to compose herself.

'Have you got hold of my husband?'

'Yes, He's on his way.'

Tim burst into the room moments later, not waiting for his knock to be acknowledged, and wrapped his arms around Sophie.

'Are you alright?'

'Just about. It's Julie I'm worried about.'

'Where is she?'

'Downstairs. The teachers thought it best for her to be with her friends while we talk. Then we can take her home, or let her stay on and try and keep everything as normal as possible.'

Tim listened carefully as she gave him a detailed account of what had happened, while Tim took notes, looking increasingly serious. He then turned to the policewoman.

'I passed the car with the forensics people all over it. Have they found anything?'

'Yes this, so far.' She passed over the photograph in a clear plastic folder.

'*Jesus*, Sophie. That's taken outside our house!'

'I know. They've obviously been stalking us. Following us to school. It's *horrific*. Why would anyone do that?'

'I think I know.'

'What? Something to do with your Dad?'

'Maybe,' said Tim grimly, 'and I bloody well intend to find out. Anyway, let's go and see Julie if we're finished here.'

For him, the situation had just got *really* personal.

CHAPTER 32

BIGHTON

'I'm bloody well going to kill him.'

Tim was sitting with his father, nursing a glass of whisky.

'Who?' asked Robin, guessing the answer.

'MacDonald, of course. Fucking so-called Big Mack.'

'For God's sake Tim, see sense!'

'Well, nobody seems to be able to stop him, or even slow him down.'

'If it *is* him,' interjected Robin.

Tim was undeterred. 'He's had a go at you twice, at Alice twice, and now he's going after *my* family – my *kid*, for God's sake! And what do you think that's done to Sophie? She's terrified of going out or even letting Julie play outside. Now *we're* living in a prison, not just him.

We've tried to warn people; we've tried to get him moved. And in spite of help from that Bloomfield woman, nothing seems to work. I seriously think he's got to be stopped physically. In fact, permanently, if I have anything to do with it.'

Robin shook his head in disbelief.

'Tim, don't be ridiculous. I know you've been through a nightmare, every parent's worst nightmare, but you're a *police* officer. You can't start taking the law into your own hands. That's crazy. And you know it. Or you ought to, in your position.'

'Why not, if no-one else will?'

'For one thing, you're supposed to be professional. Then there's a little moral issue, *and* you'd almost certainly get caught. End of your reputation. End of your career. Banged up for years.End of your life with Sophie and Julie. End of everything you've ever worked for. End of me, for that matter, or at least my respect.'

He still didn't know if Tim was really serious.

'I've thought about that. There may be ways round it.'

'So how do you propose doing it?' He still didn't believe that his own son was considering murder.

'Well, he's too big and too well-protected to try the old thing of an accident. So then, I thought about trying to poison him. But with ordinary poison, the danger is that someone else might get killed. For instance, if it was in chocolates, his prisoner pals might eat one. Or he might even offer one to a guard. So, something more selective.'

Robin was still listening very closely – but aghast. His son *was* clearly serious about this.

'Then the big raid, and its results, gave me a better idea. Why not use the one thing he *really* needs at the moment – a mobile phone? Why not doctor one and fix it to explode? It's not even a *new* idea. The Israeli Mossad have been doing that to knock off the Hezbollah and their other local enemies for years. And I've got a pal who's a real whizz at electronics, and I'm pretty sure he could rig a smart-phone to blow up the second time you dialled a number, or at least something like that.'

'Tim, for God's sake, *shut up!*' Robin had put up a hand to silence him. But his son was undeterred.

'Then, to get the phone to Mack, we could use a drone, having tipped him off that a phone would be be delivered that way. We could even be using Mack's *own* system, including the bent staff, to make it all sound realistic. Nice touch of irony!"

'I'm not listening to this, Tim. You've gone off your head. I know you and Sophie have gone through hell. We *all* have. But this is madness! And may I remind you, you have no proof that Big Mack was behind it. Just supposition. Hardly what you'd expect from a detective.'

But Tim wasn't listening.

'I've even researched the kind of four-engine drone that might work – a DJI Phantom 3. Apparently, it's very quiet, being electric. The shop I went to even admitted they get lots of requests from some very questionable people.' He smiled cynically.

'This isn't funny, Tim. You're talking like a maniac. And if you *are* serious, I want *nothing* to do with it. *Nothing*, do you hear me? I don't want you ever talking like that again. You're a policeman, not a vigilante.'

Tim fell silent, his determination undiminished. And something was about to happen, thirty-five miles to the north, which would only strengthen his resolve.

CHAPTER 33

PUTNEY

Alice turned on her bedroom television to watch the news.

'Good morning. We have breaking news at six o'clock.

There's been an explosion in London on the A3 between Putney Hill and the Kingston by-pass. We have no news of casualties, but the road has been closed in both directions. There are already huge queues building up of traffic coming into London and trying to leave. We'll be back to you as soon as we have more information.'

||||||

'The time is 6.15. We can now bring you more news of the explosion on the A3. The police and fire service are on the scene. As you can see from this helicopter shot, there's a large blackened area on the carriageway coming up the hill, and opposite a large ASDA supermarket. There are still some flames and quite a lot of smoke.

Traffic is backed up at a standstill in both directions, and drivers are strongly advised to avoid the area. We have no news about possible casualties, but it may be fortunate that this event occurred so early in the morning, before the rush hour, and before the ASDA store opened for customers.'

||||||

Our top story at 6.30, the A3 explosion. We're now getting reports that it was a Royal Mail van that exploded. However, Royal Mail say they have no vehicles unaccounted for at the moment.

The nearby ASDA supermarket reports that nearly all its windows facing the road were blown in. Fortunately, no customers were in the store, but several staff have been rushed to nearby hospitals to be treated for wounds caused by flying glass.

A bus and several cars and lorries on the A3 were also damaged, and injured drivers and passengers have also been ferried by ambulance to hospital. No fatalities are reported so far, although some are anticipated in the van.'

IIIII

'It's seven o'clock. We've now been informed that the A3 explosion is being treated as a possible terrorist attack. It's also been confirmed that the van is *not* a genuine Royal Mail vehicle, and that the bomb squad and forensic teams are now sifting through the wreckage. One theory is that the van exploded prematurely on the way to a high profile target, such as a Government building or barracks.

We've also just heard that police have been despatched to Kingston Hospital, where some of the injured were taken by ambulance.'

IIIIII

Realising that the explosion had been less than a mile away, Alice was acutely worried that some of her patients that day might be caught up in it. Which of them lived in or near Kingston? She'd have to check if they were okay. They had enough problems already without this. *What the hell was the world coming to?*

She switched off the television, appalled.

Detective Inspector John Utley of Scotland Yard's Anti-Terrorism Unit was standing in the chaotic scene on the road. All around him men and women in white forensic clothing were sifting through the wreckage. There was little to be found intact of the rear of the 'Royal Mail' van, but the engine, radiator and front suspension *were* recognisable, and the engine and chassis numbers had confirmed that it had indeed once been part of the thousands of vehicles in the Royal Mail fleet, but had recently been sold at auction. The front number plate, too, was intact, but had quickly proved to be false.

In the Transit van, there appeared to have been two occupants, although both were unrecognisable. But among the body parts sent off to the lab for DNA and other analysis were remnants of three hands – which could reveal fingerprints. The forensics team had already been able to report that the explosion was caused by a crude, but very large fertilizer bomb rather than any more sophisticated explosive like Semtex. More fingerprints could be present on pieces of bodywork from the van, and the steering wheel and gear-lever.

Across the road on the far carriageway was a red number 85 bus with most of its windows blown in, and a couple of cars and vans, one of which had slid into the back of the bus.

Utley was greatly relieved that there were no life-threatening injuries among the public, although there were a number of serious facial ones caused by flying glass, some of which were being treated by specialists at the Moorfields Eye Centre at St George's Hospital in Tooting.

There had been some strokes of luck, too, if luck were the right word. The bomb vehicle had blown up just where the ramp from under the road emerged, and on the left was a piece of wasteland. Just another few yards on, and the first of a row of houses, with their occupants, would have been hit. On the right was the ASDA supermarket tower building, its clock stopped at 5.48. Again, just another few yards and many more of the ASDA staff, stacking shelves, would have been exposed. And Utley noted something else. The A3's central barrier was made of concrete blocks that *curved* upwards from the road-base – as it happened, a perfect blast deflector. This might explain why the damage to the bus and the cars had not been even worse.

But at that moment, the Inspector was mostly intrigued by a wrecked black Ford Mondeo *on his side* of the carriageway. He estimated that it had been travelling in the slow lane only a few feet in front of the exploding van, and that the back of the vehicle had been smashed in by the blast, with the rear window blown inwards. Luckily, the fuel tank had not gone up. He'd been informed that its three injured occupants had been taken by ambulance to Kingston Hospital.

His suspicions about the car were suddenly confirmed when young Sergeant Lally received a call on his mobile. He pointed to the Mondeo's wreckage. 'Sir, they confirm this one's been stolen, too. From somewhere in Surbiton. And it's certainly been repainted. Its owner reported it as silver only a week ago.'

Inspector Utley didn't hesitate. 'Check that our people are still at Kingston Hospital, and tell them *whatever they do* to stay with the three from this vehicle. I want to know who they are. And warn them they may be dangerous. I'll join you as soon as I can.

Oh, and tell the CCTV trawl team to look for images of either of these vehicles, a red Transit looking like a Royal Mail one and a black Mondeo, especially between five forty-five and six-thirty, and *especially* driving together. Not just on the A3, but on any of the feeder roads coming on to the Kingston by-pass as far back as Esher.' He paused, calculating time and distance. 'No, even back to the M25. And Kingston itself, and Surbiton.'

Pulling on rubber gloves, he approached the Mondeo. Its doors were already open, where the paramedics had extracted the occupants. The interior was chaotic, but there was a Satnav that appeared to be still operating, and some photographs on the floor. There was also a device that he recognised as something like a model aircraft radio-controller. As he got out clutching them in his gloved hands, he was interrupted by his Sergeant proffering a mobile.

'Sir, Sergeant Foster, for you.' Utley quickly put the objects he was holding on to a plastic sheet on the ground and reached for the phone.

'Foster, where are you?'

'At the hospital, Sir. We've had the other patients moved and locked down the ward with just the three men from the Mondeo. They won't give their names, but I can tell you they're of Middle-Eastern appearance. None of them are badly injured, and one of them is kicking up a real stink, adamant about wanting to leave.'

'I *bet* he is,' said Utley. 'Well, make sure he *doesn't*. In fact, I'm sending you an Armed Response Team. Some of their friends might try to rescue them.

Read them their rights and then fingerprint them and take DNA swabs. And send the fingerprints to the team here. We'll be needing them later.'

He passed the evidence he'd found in the Mondeo to the forensics team to be checked for fingerprints and DNA, and then took them back, carefully placed in plastic evidence bags. For the following hour, he then supervised the collection of everything else of interest to be sent to the lab, including pieces of the Royal Mail identity decals that had obviously been used to make the vehicle look authentic. Pressure was mounting, because the Traffic Department was now pressuring him to open up at least one lane in each direction on such a heavily-used road.

At last, he decided he could open up the lanes, and asked his Sergeant to drive him to the hospital. Like the ambulances, his car was able to go back down the ramp, under the A3 and then back towards Kingston.

All the way there, still wearing gloves, he studied the Satnav and the photographs and puzzled over them. The radio control device's purpose was obvious enough. But why was the Satnav set to arrive in Kensington, at Derry Street? And why did all the photographs seem to be of the *Daily Mail* building?

||||||

When he reached Kingston Hospital, Inspector Utley was pleased to see a police BMW parked at the main entrance. One of its burly crew was standing by it, a sub-machine-gun slung round his neck, a not very subtle way of saying the place was guarded. When they reached the ward, the other two men of the Armed Response Unit were there, one inside the ward and the other outside, at whom one young visitor, a boy with his mother, was staring with undisguised awe and curiosity.

John Utley quickly identified himself to the Ward Sister, and asked, 'Is there another room we could use to talk to those men, where we can wheel a bed?'

She nodded, pointing to her right. 'Sure, just over there.'

'Thanks. Right, Sergeant Lally, let's get them to wheel the first fellow in there, the youngest one.'

||||||

The bed was in the middle of the ward, surrounded by curtains. For a couple of minutes John Utley waited in the entrance for another officer he had asked for, who turned out to be a dark-eyed policewoman of about twenty-five and in uniform. She was to be an Arabic translator if one were needed. Utley shook hands with her, asked her name and then whispered a briefing to his team. They then all strode over to the bed and ripped back the curtains.

The occupant of the bed was handcuffed to it. His head was bandaged, probably concealing injuries caused by the flying glass from the shattered back window of the Mondeo. He looked very young and disorientated, his eyes flicking round the room as if desperately searching for his two companions. But all he could see were two men in suits, a huge grim man in a black flak-jacket with a sub-machinegun and a young dark-skinned policewoman.

The older, suited man placed a black machine at the end of the bed and fetched a chair. He pressed the recording button.

'This is an interview at 3.30 pm on November Twelfth, 2018, conducted at Kingston Hospital. Present are Detective Inspector John Utley, Detective Sergeant James Lally, Sergeant Bill Hardy and Constable Aisha Mahmed.'

He turned to the wide-eyed figure in the bed, speaking slowly. 'What's your name?'

The young man just stared at him.

Utley nodded to Aisha to try in Arabic.

'Shoo ismak?' she asked, in a gentle voice.

'It's okay, I speak English.'

'Good' said Utley. 'But please stay anyway, Aisha.'

He turned back to the figure in the bed. 'Now, what's your name?'

||||||

The whole morning had been a revelation. First the boy – who had finally admitted he was called Muhammed Safar – was in an hysterical state, and Utley soon found out why. Apparently his older brother Ali was in the Transit and had been blown to bits. Ironic, thought Utley, in that Ali – his brother had reluctantly revealed – was meant to be the electronics 'expert' and some electronic fault undoubtedly seemed to have triggered the device prematurely.

Muhammed claimed he didn't know any of the others. They'd been summoned to a house in Surbiton and presented with the two vehicles, with him being chosen as the Ford Mondeo's driver.

According to him, there had been no expected pep talk about the purpose of the mission, and no posing for a jihadist propaganda video. And it had puzzled Muhammed as to why a newspaper seemed to be the target.

The older man who had briefed them – he had not given his name – had assured them that the mission was just a gesture and that there was not much explosive in the van. And, above all, that there was no danger. Ali Safar, preparing the bomb, must have known that was a lie, but he had mentioned nothing to his brother.

So when Ali and the van driver had been obliterated, Muhammed had just fallen apart, now rocking and crying in the hospital bed. It was now impossible to get any sense out of him. On top of that, he didn'tt seem to know much more, so after a while, Utley and his team isolated him and prepared to interview the others.

The first one appeared much more in control, but before they could start questioning him, Sergeant Lally suddenly took Utley to one side, whispering urgently.

'Sir, it's important. Elliot was able to get to the last one's locker while we were interviewing him. You might want to look at this, found in his back pocket.'

He laid out a tiny scrap of paper. It had a scrawled address on it – one in Surbiton, with a postcode.

Utley frowned, thinking. He put on rubber gloves and reached for the satnav. And sure enough, before the Derry Street route plan, there was another one – to an address in Surbiton, with a postcode.

The same one.

Christ! Quickly Utley called in to the Operations Room at Scotland Yard, explained the situation and the unexpected and unusual apparent target. He received confirmation that the Surbiton house would be quickly and quietly sealed off by an Armed Response Team. However, he was not very optimistic. After all, it was now fully three hours since the dramatic first television and radio reports would have surely revealed to the plotters that their plan had gone badly wrong.

He then briefed Sergeant Lally about his plans and what to look out for in the next two interviews, and then ran down the hospital corridor to meet a police-car which had been summoned.

Lights flashing and siren blaring, they hurtled down the hill and then hammered down the Kingston by-pass. The driver was a grey-haired Sergeant who muttered and swore under his breath as the traffic, travelling perfectly correctly and legally at 50 mph, did not get out of his way fast enough.

Near the Surbiton cut-off, Utley leaned forward to ask him to turn off the siren – in the unlikely case there might be anybody still in the house.

His phone buzzed. It was Sergeant Lally.

'Not a lot more, Sir. They spoke less English, so I had to use Aisha more. Both claim to be refugees from Syria.'

Utley grunted. He was not about to be too sympathetic to potential mass-murderers.

'Otherwise they didn't do much more than confirm the first kid's story.'

He paused. 'I don't know about you, Sir, but I think there's something very strange about all this.'

'How do you mean?' Utley almost guessed what was coming.

'Well, there's none of the fanatical pro-Islam, anti-Western stuff. They seem to be all amateurs, and it's more as if they were just a sort of scratch team pulled together to do a one-off job of work – like painting a house.'

'Right, Jim, I think I know *exactly* what you mean. And thanks for the thought. Anyway, I've got to ring off. We're near the house.'

||||||

It was a long, tree-lined street, typical of British suburbia. In fact, the very name 'Surbiton' sounded as if it had invented that kind of street. The Armed Response Officers were crouched behind the houses and in the gardens about a hundred metres from the suspect house. DI Utley came up and squatted beside the Inspector in charge, a hard-faced man dressed in black, with a flak-jacket, visored helmet and carrying an assault rifle.

'Any movement?' asked Utley.

'Nothing. We've been here half an hour. There's no sign of life and no vehicles either. And we've checked with infra-red and there are no heat sources.'

'I'm not surprised. They've had hours after the first TV pictures to make themselves scarce.'

'I'd say the birds have flown.'

'CCTV trawl?'

'Not a useful camera for miles. The neighbours say they were a quiet, middle-eastern couple, and middle-aged. But, then, there'd been a sudden lot of visitors, apparently all young men, in the last few days.'

Utley looked down the street and frowned.

'Look, I think we'd better risk going in. There may be stuff in there that I can use, and urgently.'

'Okay, but it'll be slow finding it. Even if they've gone, my specialists will have to check for booby-traps.'

'Of course.'

It *was* indeed slow, at least half an hour before the building was declared all clear. Once the armed SWAT team had checked it out, they had carefully handed over the site to Utley and to the white-coated forensics team that he had ordered in.

It was obvious to Utley that the occupants of the house had left in a considerable hurry. There was cold coffee and three half-eaten breakfasts still on the kitchen table and files and papers were scattered about everywhere. Plenty of DNA to study, but no smart-phones, no computers, just their charging cables left where equipment had been snatched away.

However, there was a big garage at the back, and it did not take long to see the remains of what looked like powdered fertilizer on the floor, probably where the 'Royal Mail' van had been loaded. And maybe the tools and tins might reveal something useful.

But then something came up – an unexpected stroke of luck. Up in one of the bedrooms there was a phone, a landline one – perhaps overlooked in the urgent rush to get out. And when Utley, on the off-chance, dialled 1471 he got the number of the 'last caller'. It was a mobile, and he noted the number, knowing its location could be traced if it was still being used. Normally terrorists would call mobile to mobile, but maybe, just maybe, this caller had tried the landline first.

There might be a way to find out.

CHAPTER 34

SCOTLAND YARD

'Bill, I need an urgent favour.' John Utley felt he had no time to go through 'normal channels'. So he was talking directly to an old friend of his in a very secret listening centre.

'Fire away, John.'

'I'm working on that big explosion on the A3. It turns out it was a terrorist operation, but a rather peculiar one. A bit sloppy and amateur – and not with the normal sort of ISIS or Al Qaeda target. *And* of course, the device went off prematurely. We tracked back to the house where it was prepared, but no-one was there. There was one possible clue, though. There was a land-line phone still there, and I got the last caller's number. A mobile. So, a question. If I give you that number, can you trace any calls on it?

'Maybe. It would depend if anything suspicious, words or names, had triggered our computers to listen. It's much easier if we know in advance, of course. Anyway, give me the number and we'll have a go. But I can't promise anything.'

||||||

In the event, it was only two hours before the call was returned.

'John, you're in luck. The caller to the landline happened to use some words that had triggered a listen-in. The first words were 'HSU', meaning High Security Unit, part of a prison. The second was 'Belmarsh'.

The call was in Arabic, but I had it translated. And listen to this.

'Ahmed, are you there? Peace be with you. I just got out of HSU, but I'm still in Belmarsh. And I've got something big for you. Lots of money. I'll call your mobile number. Goodbye.'

'Good work, Bill.'

'And that's not the end of it. The phone's *still* being used. We're now listening to it all the time. And unbelievably, it's being used in a prison.'

'I wish you surprised me'

'And one which, sure enough, *does* have an HSU.'

'Where?'

'Belmarsh, as that caller mentioned, down in Woolwich. Someone else is using it now, to order drugs and things. Sounds British, maybe Scottish – certainly not Arabic.'

||||||

Utley's next call was to the Duty Governor at Belmarsh. After he'd explained the situation about the A3 explosion, he asked if there had been any prisoner from the Middle-East released in the last two weeks from the High Security Unit to the main blocks.

After a few moments, the Governor came back on the line.

'Yes, we have a Kassim Nazari. He's the only one in the time-frame of the call. In for terrorist offences and incitement to violence.'

'I'd like to come and interview him, if I may. Tomorrow, if possible.'

'Fine, I'll make sure he's available, without alerting him.'

'Thanks, that's very helpful. Just one other thing. Wasn't there a big thing about Belmarsh, you know, in one of the papers?'

'Certainly was, I'm afraid. Two weeks ago. Caused no end of trouble. Hell of a stink. We had a huge raid here, ordered by the Ministry. Found loads of drugs, and of course, phones.'

'So, for a while, the prisoners would have been cut off?'

'For several days at least.'

'So a phone would have been something precious?'

'Absolutely. Gold dust.'

'Thanks. I'll see you tomorrow then. About eleven.'

IIIIII

The next morning, John Utley was just putting on his coat when there was a knock on his door. It was his friend and colleague DI Joe Bain from down the passage.

'Can I have a quick word, John?'

'Sure.'

'I heard that you were off down to Belmarsh. Something about your bomb investigation?'

'That's right.'

'I've got a special interest in that place. Goes right back to Robin Marshal's time.'

John Utley remembered Robin with fondness and respect. Like Joe Bain, he'd been part of his very successful team in the early days and Robin had been something of a mentor to him.

'There's a prisoner there called MacDonald, nick-named 'Big Mack'. May seem a funny name, but the reality is far from funny. He's one of those Caesars, and we suspect he's very dangerous – even for those on the outside. Tip me off if anyone mentions him.'

'Certainly will.'

CHAPTER 35

WANDSWORTH

Tim Marshal had asked his superiors if he could take some leave. They were very understanding, naturally assuming that he wanted to be with his family after the horrifying incident and the threat to his daughter Julie outside her school.

In fact, Tim had suggested Sophie and Julie should take a complete break at Sophie's mother's house in the country in Sussex. It was now the school holiday and Julie adored her grandmother, and there was a dog there that she loved. Both of them agreed that it would take the little girl's mind off things. So Tim was now free to work alone. And he had not spoken to his father for several days, after they had parted on decidedly edgy terms.

He had a big garage alongside their old house in Earlsfield, but never kept his car in it. Instead, it was devoted to his hobby. He unlocked the side-door and switched on the lights. Hanging from the ceiling were several large model aircraft, nearly all of which he had built himself. Mostly they were single-engined, but there was one twin – a Mosquito. There were also two helicopters, a Huey and an Apache, nicely painted in American Marine Corps colours, and several drones of various sizes, together with the transmitters.

But Tim concentrated on the box on the floor that had just been delivered by Parcel Force. He carefully slit open the top, opened the box and removed the extensive polystyrene packaging. The DJI Phantom 3 was revealed, with four propellers and finished in glossy white. He noted that he would need to re-paint over the shiny livery with matt black or dark grey. He checked the camera, for which the drone was a sophisticated photographic platform. He would certainly be needing that. He now started to charge the battery for the machine and settled down to read the Operating Manual carefully. Tomorrow he would take the drone out and learn to fly it. And then he would need to make some calls.

IIIIII

He took the whole morning flying the drone in the park. After a while he got the hang of it, and using the monitor screen on the controller, was able to guide it accurately and into small spaces. He noted with satisfaction that, with its four electric motors, it flew in virtual silence.

Tim got home in time for a sandwich lunch and another look through the Operating Manual. He'd have to practise at least once more – and, he reminded himself, in poor light conditions.

Late that afternoon, Tim saw a rather old Volvo stop and park across the street.

He had often wondered if his father would approve of some of his friends, or to be more accurate, 'useful acquaintances'. Certainly Aaron would fit that description. About thirty-five, almost the epitome of a 'computer nerd' – single, pale and plump from taking no exercise since he left his Youth Offender Programme. Tim was at the door before he could ring the bell and ushered him into the house rather quickly, knowing it might be better in the future if people did *not* remember his strange visitor. Tim offered him coffee or tea, but Aaron opted for a drink.

'I got what you wanted,' he announced, sitting down heavily on the sofa, then opening up a rather battered briefcase and holding up a mobile phone.

'It's a standard-looking iPhone, with some modifications. I've replaced the battery with a smaller one, and then used the spare battery space for five grams of Semtex and a micro detonator. I've then programmed the phone to switch on normally, and to make any dialled number. Then after five seconds, the time normally taken from dialling to lifting a phone to your ear, it'll trigger the detonator and explode.'

He held up the phone, and Tim noticed for the first time that he was wearing gloves. 'It's a tiny amount of explosive, but next to someone's ear, it'll be quite enough.' He smirked. 'I suggest you take my word for it, and don't have a trial run.'

Tim stared at him, not reacting at first, in a whirlwind of conflicting emotions. Here he was, a respected police Sergeant, from a police family, and he was cold-bloodedly discussing a murder method with an extremely dubious character whose underworld connections he knew and now even valued. He knew he should be ashamed, but wasn't.

'Well done, Aaron. And have another glass. And here's the money.' He handed over a wad of notes. Aaron, took off his gloves, counted them methodically and then looked up.

'Thank you. And, by the way, lock that thing away. You really don't want your kids trying out Daddy's new phone. Even *I* got a bit worried just bringing it here.'

It was with some relief that Tim watched his visitor amble across the road and drive away. He then wiped the phone down to remove any fingerprints. He'd have to do the same with the drone, of course, in case it crashed. Now he had to set in motion the plan that would have 'Big Mack' expecting a precious phone, and knowing that it would be flown into Belmarsh by drone. A Sunday night would be best, he thought – much less traffic and far fewer people around.

The next few days saw Tim Marshal in a heightening state of anxiety. As the immediate fury about the attack on his daughter subsided a little, he wondered if he was doing the right thing taking the law into his own hands, but doing nothing was too much for him. There was no doubt what his father thought about it, and he was pretty sure that Sophie would be equally horrified. And he certainly wasn't going to confide in her.

But he was still very angry and frustrated. Here was a convicted criminal, theoretically safely locked up to protect the public, but the reality was that the system had completely failed to stop him organising the killing of innocent people – and even from *inside* a jail, for God's sake! Tim decided to proceed with his plan.

After several practise sessions, he was now very proficient at flying the drone, and was sure he could get it to the specific window at Belmarsh's B Block. Wearing gloves, he retrieved the iPhone and put it in the carrying pouch, ready to be attached under the body of the Phantom – which was now painted a matt dark grey. Through some highly unsavoury underworld connections, Tim had fixed that Big Mack would be expecting the drone delivery at his window on a specific Sunday night, courtesy of someone Mack thought he knew.

Tim then borrowed a car from a friend, saying his own was in for service. He certainly didn't want his own car or number plates showing up on any of the thousands of CCTV cameras. Police would be CCTV 'trawling' intensively, especially in South London, now a very sensitive area, ever since that bomb had gone off on the A3, creating massive police activity for several days. For good measure, he changed the number plates on the borrowed car to some he had obtained from a scrap metal merchant who owed him a favour.

Then, at about seven in the evening, he set off on his mission.

CHAPTER 36

DUXFORD, CAMBRIDGE

A Mark Nine Spitfire flew low over the motorway, the flaps and wheels in its unmistakable elliptical wings already down for landing. The canopy was slid back and the pilot visible.

'*I'd love to be flying that, rather than driving a bus,*' smiled Jimmy Oliver, looking up though the windscreen. He'd passed Duxford so many times on his routine delivery trips to Whitemoor Prison, but hadn't gone into the aerodrome or seen an air show for years, even though he'd always loved old planes. Perhaps if he'd had a son there might have been more of a reason, or an excuse, to go. Certainly Maureen wouldn't be interested, nor his daughter or grand-daughter.

Moments later, the grey prison transport vehicle reached the M11 motorway turn-off for Duxford and its famous aerodrome, and Jimmy was surprised to see a police car at the beginning of the exit slip-road, its blue lights flashing.

A police officer was waving him down, and pointing for him to take the slip-road. Maybe there was some kind of emergency? A crash? An air accident? Jimmy slowed down, pulled over and stopped. The officer walked over and Jimmy opened the window.

He was appalled to find himself staring down the barrel of a gun.

'Switch off, open the door and *don't* try anything!'

Jimmy was terrified, and certainly *not* going to try anything. They were only a *private* company, contracted to transport prisoners round the country. He might be wearing a uniform, but he wasn't a prison officer or even a civil servant. He was near retirement – and had a wife and daughter to get back to in Chingford. There was going to be no dramatic bravery from *him*.

He duly switched off, called his colleagues as calmly as possible, then opened the door and slowly climbed down. Frightened though he was, he couldn't help taking in the realism of the 'police' uniform, even though the man had a huge disguising moustache. And the 'police-car', with its flashing lights, red stripes and all, was pretty realistic, too.

The middle door now opened and out came the two other escorting officers, younger fellows, who flinched when they saw the situation, but obediently filed down with their hands up – and then came the one prisoner, the big fellow they'd been warned about.

'Put your hands *down*,' said one of the other two 'policemen' who had emerged from the car, obviously worried about drawing any extra attention from the passing motorists driving down the slip-road off the motorway.

'Give me *that*,' growled Big Mack, wrenching the pistol from the man who'd stopped the prison van.

He then turned, suddenly.

And shot Jimmy and each of the other prison officers once in the chest.

He walked calmly away towards the car.

'What the *fuck* did you do *that* for?' blurted one of his rescuers, gaping with shock.

'Shut up, and get in the car,' snarled Big Mack.

'Jesus, we'll *all* be marked men. *That* wasn't part of the deal.'

The doors all slammed shut. 'Christ!'

'JUST FUCKIN' DRIVE!' shouted Mack, the pistol waving maniacally in his hand.

CHAPTER 37

BELMARSH PRISON

If asked, John Utley would have to admit that Belmarsh gave him the creeps. Even though most of the inmates might have got what they deserved, it was still thoroughly depressing. Incredibly bleak from the outside, inside was even worse. He would far prefer to have been on home ground or even next door in Woolwich Police Station.

Now he sat in the interview room, with a file and a tape recorder in front of him on the desk. And sitting on a metal and canvas chair in front of him was Kassim Nazari. He was a grey-haired Arab with a neat beard. Considering his position, he seemed quite relaxed. Perhaps he knew things that Utley and Belmarsh didn't.

And it was quite soon, after a series of 'routine' questions that Utley decided it was safe enough not to waste any more time before trying to cut a deal. But before he could go down that route, his thoughts were suddenly interrupted.

'It was Mack that made me do it.'

John Utley looked up from his notes, startled. 'Who?'

'Big Mack, in B Block.'

He tried not to look too interested. 'Who's he?'

'The king around here. I'm surprised you don't know that. Everyone else does.

But he promised me many things for my family, and much money. Told me to get the Brothers to attack a newspaper. Much easier than going for the government or the military. Or the police, come to that.' He smirked.

Utley stared at him and got up.

'I am terminating this interview, for the moment. DI Utley left the room at eleven fifty-six.' He switched off the recorder.

As Utley strode to the door, Kassim Nazari looked at him in surprise. What on earth had he said?

Once he was out of the door, Utley turned to the Duty Governor. 'I need to interview this MacDonald fellow at once.'

A Principal Officer left the room, presumably to make a call. Utley sat down, thinking hard.

A few minutes later, a tall, smartly-dressed woman entered the ante-room and introduced herself. 'Inspector Utley, I'm Mary Bloomfield, Deputy Governor. I understand you want to see the prisoner, MacDonald?'

'Yes, we think he may be involved in the explosion in Putney.'

'Really?' She looked puzzled. *How?* And *why?*

'Anyway, I'm afraid you can't see him. At least, not here. He was moved early this morning. And without warning, so he couldn't organise anything before he left. I'd been recommending it for some time, to break the links with his power-base. He'd been running all sorts of things from here. That's clearly why there was that raid. But at last they found him a place at Whitemoor. You could go and see him there. It's near Cambridge, as you probably know.'

She turned to the Principal Officer.

'Mr Wood, can you please call Whitemoor and see if MacDonald's arrived.'

Mary Bloomfield was describing some of the problems they'd had with MacDonald, when Wood burst back into the room, looking very flustered.

'He hasn't turned up at Whitemoor, Marm, and they've lost

radio contact with the transport. A full-scale escape alert has just been initiated.'

Whatever Mary might have been about to say was drowned out by alarms going off all over the prison. Then her mobile rang. She listened, ashen-faced.

'Christ! Jessop, MacDonald's cell-mate, has just had his ear blown off – by a phone!'

|||||||

John Utley and Mary Bloomfield were not the first to hear the news about Duxford. A passing motorist had posted his picture of the bodies on YouTube and the world knew.

And at Belmarsh the phones began ringing.

They were all gathered in a conference room, trying to work out which priorities to deal with first. The Cambridge police had called to confirm that all three of the escorting officers were dead, each shot once in the chest at close range. None had been armed – so it was unprovoked murder. Cartridge cases had been recovered and gunshot residue found on the clothing, and the bodies had been removed for post-mortem tests. There would certainly be CCTV coverage at that important junction, but it had not been recovered and analysed yet.

There were also strange reports by several members of the public of a police car near the scene earlier, but Cambridge reported they were absolutely adamant that none of their cars were there at the time.

The shaken Belmarsh group was just deciding who should have the terrible task of breaking the totally unexpected news to the families of the victims, when the National Offender Management Service came on the line.

'Lionel Hawkins here, NOMS.' He sounded very agitated over

the loudspeaker. 'The Justice Secretary's just been on to me. She was extremely shaken, and I can hardly blame her. What on earth's happening? Who were they escorting? I suppose the van was going to Whitemoor? Am I right?'

Mary Bloomfield was handed the phone, feeling as if it were a 'poisoned chalice'. She started to explain that a prisoner, a long-suspected trouble-maker, was being moved to Whitemoor.

'Was he the fellow the *Daily Mail* article was hinting about?'

'Yes, probably. His name's James Dougal MacDonald, in for attempted murder. Seven years to run. We knew he was the prime-mover in a drugs racket here, so we wanted to move him out to break the hold on his power-base. He was the only prisoner being moved on that transport, so it looks as if it was him, or his accomplices, who murdered those poor transport officers. All from a transport service company, not even prison officers. If it was *that* cold-blooded, it certainly looks as if it might be MacDonald himself.'

'Good God! But why wasn't he escorted by *armed* officers?'

'Well, because on paper, he was a model prisoner. Never put a foot wrong. Or to be more accurate, none we could ever nail him for. Far too clever. Even had 'enhanced prisoner' status. We ourselves only ever knew by very indirect hearsay what he was up to, or that he was running the main drug business. We hoped your big raid would catch him, but he was much too smart. Another inmate took the rap for his phone, and of course it had been wiped. And nobody talked, of course. He scared everyone rigid. Frankly, it's why we had to get him moved.'

'Well, the media are all over this. We've had a hell of a job fighting them off. I dread Channel Four News in a few minutes, it's always so much longer and more detailed.'

Mary took the decision not to tell the plainly rattled boss of NOMS about the incident of Big Mack's cell-mate, until it could be checked out properly. But John Utley had realized at once that he should tell Joe Bain in Scotland Yard what had happened to the man he seemed so interested in. He quietly moved to the corner of the room and dialled his mobile phone. Joe sounded very anxious, but Utley was not to know the real reason why.

'You're not going to *believe* this, but Mack's escaped.' Only minutes later Joe was passing on the news to Robin Marshal.

'John Utley, you remember him, is investigating that Putney bomb incident. And there's a connection with Belmarsh. And he's just told me the news. That the escaped prisoner was Mack, up at Duxford. You know, where the three escorting officers were killed. He was being moved from Belmarsh to Whitemoor. And mad, vindictive bastard that he is, I'll bet he was the one who actually pulled the trigger. And probably for no reason.'

'Christ! So he's on the loose now, and he was dangerous enough locked up. I'd better tell Alice. She'll freak – and so she should. And then there's Tim.' Robin thought that at least Tim would not be going ahead with any mad-cap schemes to kill Mack now.

||||||

The Duxford atrocity had many consequences. The media, of course, had a field day. They were able to focus on Big Mack as a perfect symbol of what people thought was wrong with Britain's prisons. How he had been able to almost 'rule' a prison was bad enough, but the way he was able to escape made it much worse.

In the House of Commons, the next Wednesday's 'Prime Minister's Question Time' was thoroughly embarrassing for the Government. MP after Opposition MP stood up to tear into the Prime Minister, who clearly found enormous difficulty in responding. So it was almost inevitable that there would be a political casualty, which unsurprisingly turned out to be the Justice

Minister, who soon resigned. It was a little unfair on her, bearing in mind the budget cuts and the loss of so many experienced prison officers, but in the fraught circumstances a scapegoat had to be found.

The early retirement of the Governor of Belmarsh made little difference, too. The same abuses continued, as they did in most prisons.

For Alice and Robin Marshal, the disappearance of 'Big Mack' for many weeks might have been a relief.

But not for long.

CHAPTER 38

BIGHTON

'So that bastard 'Big Mack' sent something to you, too?'

Alice nodded. 'Yes, yesterday'. She had driven to Robin's house as soon as she was able to clear her commitments. He couldn't help noticing that she looked strained and deathly pale. And with a look of fear in those violet eyes.

Months had passed, with absolutely no news as to where 'Big Mack' had gone. There had been plenty of speculation in the media of course, and also of political posturing too. But nothing concrete – until now.

Alice slid a clear plastic folder across the table. In it were an envelope and a beer mat.

Tim reached over, picked it up and looked at the contents carefully through the plastic.

'Yes, the same as the ones we got. A letter posted in Brazil with a McDonald's mat and an identical message; 'I'M COMING BACK TO GET YOU'.'

He paused for a moment. 'You might as well give it to me, Alice, and I'll get our lab to check it out with mine and Dad's, although so far they've found nothing to help. Yes, fingerprints on the envelopes, but probably only those of postal workers. And the three mats were all completely clean. He's far too clever not to wear gloves.'

Alice sighed. 'I'm afraid they'll find my prints all over everything. I thought it was from a girlfriend on holiday in Brazil.

I got more careful once I'd opened the envelope, but any evidence is probably ruined.'

Robin Marshal shook his head despairingly. 'Brazil? That's where that bloody Ronnie Biggs holed out for years. A pretty easy place to go to ground.'

There was a long silence while all three of them digested the concept of someone hiding out for years, but still a constant threat; not only able to threaten them from Belmarsh, but now from thousands of miles away.

Robin was the first to speak. 'It's really incredible. Three of us, all more or less in the law enforcement establishment – and all being threatened by a murderous maniac from thousands of miles away. And with no-one apparently able to do anything about it, let alone us.'

He paused, before adding, 'And up to now, we've been saved by the stupidity and incompetence of the people he sent to do us in. If Mack tries to do it *himself*, we may have even more to worry about.'

'As for me, well, I certainly can't move again. As you know, Pam's gradually getting worse, and another move would kill her. And on top of that, we've at least got all the right equipment here and the local NHS people are brilliant. I guess I'll just have to keep that gun close – the one you helpfully pointed out is illegal, Tim. Legal or illegal, so be it. But what about you, Alice?'

'I may be luckier. John's just been offered a job in Australia, with his ad agency – in their Sydney office. He wasn't sure what to do, or whether I'd go with him. But that letter from Brazil makes it far more likely I will. I don't know whether I have the right qualifications to practise there, or whether the Sydney police would be remotely interested in my work there, but it's probably the right decision to get out now. Anything's better than watching one's back all day, and not knowing whether you'll see the one after.'

She laughed, but mirthlessly. 'And there's my Dad to think about.

He's starting to find things difficult, and says that the climate in France isn't much better than here – at least for several months, especially up a mountain. Would you believe, they had fourteen inches of snow this year where he is? No-one could go anywhere for days on end. Bloody dangerous for someone of his age, being holed up like that. I know he'd like some winter warmth for his old bones, so we might *all* go. Frankly, I can't see much alternative.' She paused, and then changed the subject.

'You know something, when I heard about that Belmarsh cell-mate of Mack's having his ear blown off by a phone delivered by a drone, well, for a moment, I suspected John. He was angry enough, obsessed really, about Mack trying to do us in – and you, Robin – and, of course, his unusual hobby was flying model aircraft. In fact, I confronted him with my suspicions and he laughed and said he'd love to have tried it, but apart from anything else, he was in Milan that night, presenting to Gucci. But you have to wonder who it might have been.'

'A drink, anyone?' asked Tim suddenly, jumping up. 'I think we could all do with one.'

When she finally went back to her car, Alice felt sad more than worried about what the future held. Sydney was such a long way away – a risk of a completely different type than she would face in England, but a risk nonetheless.

And Robin, returning to the house, felt equally dejected, contemplating a fraught and threatening retirement, something he had tried so hard to avoid.

Tim, too, was similarly downcast, wondering whether he could work effectively at all while constantly worried about the safety of his family, and occasionally questioning whether if he, like Alice, should move to the other end of the world and make a fresh start.

Rage suddenly overcame him.

Why should someone, *anyone*, be able to threaten so many

lives and force such change upon them, or make their day-to-day existence so unbearable?

In the past, his wife always answered the doorbell. Not any more, unless she knew exactly who was outside. Not since the incident outside the school. And now she often kept the curtains drawn downstairs and had to be woken from nightmares. Also, she was so protective about Julie that their daughter, too, was becoming frustrated and unhappy. These days she was barely allowed to play in the garden, constantly watched and supervised, and to a suffocating extent. No longer free to go off and feed the ducks down the road in the Thames, as she always used to with her friends. In fact, rapidly becoming a prisoner as 'Big Mack' used to be, constantly frustrated by her limited freedoms, while her friends were allowed so much more. And continually phoned by her mother to see if she was okay, on the rare occasions she was out without her. In fact, she'd learned to switch off her mobile to avoid the endless calls. And that panicked her mother even more.

This couldn't go on. It was becoming intolerable.

'Mind if I have another glass, Dad?'

'No, help yourself. After all, you're not driving home.'

'No, but I wonder whether I ought to.'

There was a pause, as father and son stared into the fire.

'By the way, it was good of those people in Belmarsh to call the phone thing an accident, wasn't it?' smiled Robin. 'And that Bill fellow wasn't going to complain. Too frightened, I suppose.'

Tim looked sheepish. He realized his father had guessed for some time of his failed vigilante effort with the drone. But he'd never brought it up – until now.

'Obviously your tech friend had under-estimated the thickness of these people's skulls. Not enough explosive. So you might not have been able to knock off Mack anyway.' He grinned. 'Enough said, let's have another drink.'

CHAPTER 39

PUTNEY

'I had an email from Alice today,' said Liz to Derek over supper, 'and I'm a bit worried. Reading between the lines, she doesn't seem too happy.'

'Really? About what?'

'I'll go and fetch it.'

Seconds later she was back.

'Darling Liz,

I know we've talked a bit on Skype and I've sent a few emails, but I thought a proper 'situation report' was overdue! Well, we've all settled in, although settled isn't quite the right word as far as I'm concerned. The flat's pleasant enough, in an attractive part of Sydney, but frankly a bit small for all three of us, particularly with Dad watching sport all day with the TV on at full blast! I'd forgotten (or I didn't realize) how deaf he's becoming– and he has terrible problems putting in his hearing aids – like so many people of his age – and clearly resenting it when I try and help him as if I'm invading his personal space. And I always have to make sure he's taken them out at night, with his bedroom slap next to ours and our paper-thin walls! Frankly, I can't see us staying out here, at least without moving.

There is a small garden – well, more like a terrace – but I can still hear the telly on all day from there. And when he isn't watching sport here on TV, he's off watching it live with John, and as you know I'm not into rugby or cricket, both of which seem to obsess everyone here.

They keep asking me to go with them, but once was enough! And I'll never understand another game here they call 'Aussie Rules'.

In case you think I'm exaggerating about their worship of sport here, John Howard, their former Prime Minister, has just said 'the second most important job in Australia is Captain of Australia's cricket team'. Would you believe it?

And a famous writer apparently once described sport as 'Australia's first form of foreign policy', probably because like other countries with smallish populations they don't really have much influence on world affairs. Any meeting here, on any subject, starts with twenty minutes about some local match.

Really nice seeing Josie again, and her partner, but a bit worried they're now asking me to babysit for Amy a bit too often. It's lovely seeing their daughter, but I'm really busy revising to pass the exams to be able to practise here. Quite why I have to take them all over again is still a mystery, and bloody irritating; and now I have to take yet another one on Aboriginal culture. Apparently, Aboriginals still have a major problem with assimilating and settling, being nomadic people – and not least with alcohol and depression. So more work!

All in all, a bit of an uphill battle – as if I've gone right back to being a student after all these years!

On the plus side, the weather's great, and the people are very nice and very friendly, although their informality makes them have an infuriating habit of trying to shorten everyone's names. Would you believe, mine is often shortened to Al!'

"No worries!" is one of their favourite sayings. I must say, I'd certainly worry if I couldn't handle a couple of syllables! We've got a friend here called Haydon, a bit of a hero in flying circles here as he flew Spitfires in the war. He told us that, as soon as he arrived, he was asked; "What do you want to call yourself? Hay, or Don?" He had to choose Don. Honestly!

I have to say the art scene is terrific, really buzzy, although our flat is already decorated and furnished, and we don't have room for any more pictures.

And the wine scene is excellent, with terrific drive-through centres. We had a really good trip to Hunter Valley, quite close to here, and stocked up our mini cellar – although the wines were quite expensive. Though I have to be careful, otherwise I'll never pass those exams!

Anyway, I mustn't moan. Anything to be away from England and the reach of Big Mack and his cronies. At least I can sleep here, even though that's difficult with Dad snoring in the bedroom next door. Still, John and I are off to the Whitsunday Islands on our own pretty soon, so I can get a good kip there. Just hope that Dad can look after himself for a bit, but we really need a bit of time on our own.'

Liz paused for a sip of wine.

'Doesn't sound too brilliant,' said Derek.

'No but it gets a bit better.'

On a more cheerful note, the food scene here is utterly amazing, because of the incredible mix of nationalities: Chinese, Japanese, American, Italian, Spanish, Indonesian, Mexican – you name it. It's not expensive either, so we can go out quite a lot, which suits me fine after revising all day. And the 'fusion food' is an absolute eye-opener, and there's an amazing 'cooking library' down the road where you can photocopy recipes and sometimes see live demonstrations. When I'm not revising I try and pop in there; an idea that we really should have back home. And Manley Beach is terrific, one of my favourite places. Although I have to be really careful about sun-cream, as most people are here. That SLIP! SLOP! SLAP! campaign seems to have really worked, although I've heard about 2,000 Australians still die of skin cancer every year.Horrendous.

On the subject of baring flesh, we're halfway through a huge event here, the annual 'Gay and Lesbian Mardi Gras'. A whole month, would you believe! We've never seen anything like it, with literally thousands of people whooping it up, day and night. It makes our Gay Pride march in London seem almost tame!

Talking about London, I really miss it – and you. Making new friends, but not the same as old ones. Maybe you get to an age where that's harder, or perhaps the difference in culture gets in the way. I certainly feel I have to shut up rather more than I ever did in England, in case I offend sensibilities and people's fears that the English somehow feel superior, and I mustn't appear to be a 'whingeing Pom', as they like to put it!

The biggest feeling I have here is being so cut off, being thousands of miles away from anything I've ever known. Does anyone ever get used to that? I suppose they must, but sometimes I feel I'm on another planet. If I were here for just a few months, it wouldn't worry me, but I fear we may be here for years, and that I might even have to change my name. To Sheila, probably! And 'Diamond' may have to go for both Dad and me, to make us untraceable, even from Brazil.

Anyway, much love to you both. I'd love to hear from you. Frankly, feeling a bit lost at times.

Alice xx'

P.S. Just heard some terrific news from home a few minutes ago. My Putney house has at last been rented out in spite of its notoriety, so we can afford to move to something bigger here. Another upheaval, but this time one I'd welcome.

Derek sat back in his chair.

'Well, at least that last bit's good news. But I agree, she doesn't seem that happy otherwise. Bit of a backward step for her, if not for John. And if she's not into sport, it's going to be all the more difficult, particularly if she can't even work yet. But to be honest, I can't see us going all the way to Australia to cheer her up, however much we'd want to. Far too far away.'

'Maybe she'll adjust in time.'

'Maybe, but I can't see it - at least, not easily. Alice's just not an Australian sort of person, from what little I know about them. Too introverted. On the surface she's lively, but pretty serious underneath. Probably needing an older culture, a bit more restraint, a bit more formality in an older country like this.'

'Perhaps we should ask her over here for a bit.'

'That's crazy. She only left this country 'cos she was scared to be found by Big Mack. She's not going to come back until he's tracked down, that's if he ever is. And if she ever does come back she certainly can't stay here. I can't have you and Marcus put at risk.'

'But don't they think Big Mack;s hiding out in Brazil?'

'Yes, but he'll have cronies here.'

'I suppose so. So, she's exiled indefinitely.'

'Let's hope not.'

CHAPTER 40

VILLA MAGNA

There was a pleasant breeze, the Levante, coming off the sea, which made the temperature up the mountain quite comfortable. 'Big Mack' sat in a deckchair by the pool, nursing a beer, and felt pleasantly cool, both physically and mentally.

Things could scarcely have gone better, he mused. The escape from the prison van had turned out perfectly, although he now had misgivings about shooting those prison officers. Looking back, he now knew that was a step too far. Maybe they'd just become the focus of years of his locked-up rage.

Now, in 'retirement', he reminded himself that he *must* try to keep his temper in check. It had always been his weak point – and the source of most of his trouble. It had certainly complicated his escape from England, with his helpers now scared stiff that they were all marked men – all thought of as murderers, while he was dubbed by the media as 'the most wanted man in Britain'. The most wanted he may have been, but his disguise as a ship-hand had worked fine in Harwich, and then the false passport at Schipol and the other airports. In spite of technology, the police and border force weren't nearly as efficient as they thought they were.

And now his changed appearance would make life much easier. The brutal bald head was now covered with a full head of hair; black tinged with grey. The moustache had gone too, and his two recent dental implants had filled in the noticeable gaps in his front teeth. And his weight was now pretty normal for his height, no longer the sweaty hulk it used to be. In fact, when he looked in the mirror, he could hardly recognize himself, making it increasingly unlikely anyone else would either, especially foreign policemen.

He was no long 'Big Mack', more like 'Slim Jim'. Indeed, Jim Doyle was now what he called himself – forgettable enough one-syllable names. And foreigners wouldn't detect the difference between a Scot and an Irishman.

He had rarely smiled at his own reflection. Now he did.

And what a contrast, he thought, between here and Belmarsh! Beautiful weather, hot sunshine most of the year. A shower to himself, indeed a whole *villa* to himself. Good food and drink, a warm sea lapping a lovely beach. Cafés, bars and restaurants. And lots of women and girls, and boys for that matter – sun-tanned and gorgeous. All there for the taking, if you had the money. And Mack had plenty of that, stashed in three local banks where he seemed to be a valued and respected client.

He had carefully cultivated the image of a retired businessman, a ruse that had worked so well that salesmen from both Los Monteros and Sotogrande had even tried to sell him expensive golf course villas – clearly considering him a likely client.

He'd even been invited to join the local club – although he knew that no such invitation would have been offered to him when those aristocratic Germans in the old days had been in charge. But the Russians, they were something else. They had few qualms about members as long as you had money. After all, their own vast wealth had usually come from questionable origins.

Although it paid to be cautious, he didn't feel in danger. And he was pretty pleased with himself for cooking up the idea of his pal in Rio de Janeiro posting those letters to Marshal, his son and that bitch of a shrink. And then getting the newspapers to repeat the idea that he was in Brazil. It really helped that Ronnie Biggs, the 'Great train robber', had escaped and had lived it up there for years, flaunting a glamorous life-style that implied that 'crime *does* pay'.

In spite of the way that British police liked to try and catch British villains in Spain, he thought he had covered his tracks bloody well. And his money meant he was protected by dubious locals – British and Spanish. He had changed his name and appearance and had adopted a quiet, respectable persona.

Above all, everyone thought he was five thousand miles away in South America.

He looked at his watch. Time to meet some pals in the local bar, and collect something important.

||||||

It was just a short walk downhill into a quiet Marbella side-street and an old bar called Los Reyes, The Kings.

'Hi, Jim. Fancy a beer?'

Mack's drinking pals all suspected that he wasn't Jim Doyle, but were happy to go along with the name. After all, most of them had changed their names, too.'Enrique, un San Miguel para el Señor Doyle, por favor.'

It was difficult to work out whether his new 'friends' genuinely liked him. They certainly respected him, even probably feared him, but might never be entirely comfortable with him. And who cared? Certainly not Mack.

He settled into his usual seat and waited for his beer and, more important, for his new passport. This very soon arrived with Steve Handley, who provided most of the 'paperwork' for this very dubious community. He'd served time after being finally nailed for years of forgery back in Birmingham, but was only too pleased that his skills were still in demand.

Steve also ordered a beer and then produced an envelope from his pocket. Mack got to his feet and went outside to examine Steve's handiwork in the bright sunshine. He had to admit it was excellent, with a photograph of Mack that made him almost unrecognisable from prison days. The passport also appeared to be well-used, and issued several years ago.

When he returned to his seat, it was Mack's turn to produce an envelope.

'Well done, mate.' Steve didn't count the money, but got to his feet, nodded at the others and left.

'So, when are you going?' asked 'Titch' Jones, a tiny Welshman who always wore dark glasses even in the gloom of Los Reyes. Probably someone else with things to hide.

'I dunno,' Mack grunted. 'Sometime at the end of the month. I'm waiting for some information.' He sipped his beer, thinking.

'If you ask me,' blurted Titch, 'I think it's daft. Risking things back there when you've got it so good here.'

Mack turned, eyes narrowed, looking furious at his casual, though correct, assumption of his murky past. 'Well, I didn't fuckin' ask you, Titch. Why don't you mind your own bloody business!' Mack was suddenly displaying the menace that had made him so feared. Titch went very quiet, until Mack remembered the promise he'd made to himself about his temper and relented. A free drink might smooth things. He beckoned the barman.

'Un San Miquel para el Señor Jones, por favor!'

||||||

As he walked uphill back to the villa, Mack wondered if that irritating little Welshman had a point. After years in Belmarsh, this town was a paradise, although it *could* become a boring one, where no-one ever looked at him, let alone looked *up* to him.

But more important, he still hated that bloody policeman for sending him to Belmarsh, and for so long, and had sworn to get even.

And it was time he did.

CHAPTER 41

VILLA MAGNA

Mack now had the information he needed. Robin Marshal had not moved house, almost certainly because of the wheelchair-bound wife that Mack knew about. Still in that quiet little house in the countryside, and with no real protection. An oldish man and a cripple. Easy targets, especially as this time he wasn't going to rely on idiots to do the work. The Marshal son, however, might be more of a problem. A tough fellow with an equally tough ex-police wife. He'd figure out how to do *them* when he'd consulted with a few people.

As for the shrink bitch, she seemed to have disappeared, with the neighbours talking about Australia. He'd have to find out more when he got to Britain.

His travel plans were complete. He checked his Louis Vuitton suitcase in the hall and his leather briefcase, full of documents. And then himself in the mirror. Just the right image. Dressed smartly as a businessman, he'd fly from Malaga that afternoon to Paris Charles de Gaulle and then change to the Eurostar train, First Class, under the Channel to London. Security on the trains was always less rigorous than at the airports, especially late at night. And anyway, he was pretty sure that nobody was now looking very hard for him, except perhaps on flights from Brazil.

He decided to have one last swim, his usual thirty lengths, then shower and get ready for Manuel to drive him to the airport. Changing into his swimming trunks – now pleasingly too big for him – and gathering up a towel, he went downstairs in his two-storey annexe and out to the pool, noticing that the villa owner had thoughtfully rolled the cover back and even tossed a lilo into the pool in case he wanted a water-borne siesta.

Half an hour later, he was lugging himself on to it when he suddenly felt a dagger-sharp sting under his left arm, near the armpit – and seconds later, another one, just below.

Wasps!

Bloody irritating, he thought. And stupid of him. He'd forgotten that crevices in a lilo could provide ideal drinking troughs for parched insects frightened to rest on open water.

But in about twenty minutes, pain and irritation turned to fear. Suddenly he felt strange – curiously dizzy and disorientated – barely able to hold on to the lilo, let alone clamber on top.

What on earth was happening? He'd been stung by a wasp before. Was it the fact he'd been stung *twice*? Surely this couldn't be – what was the word? Yes, anaphylaxis, or something like that. Whatever it was, it was absolutely terrifying.

Still grasping on to the lilo as best as he could, he tried to kick towards the steps, but all at once his legs didn't seem to be working properly, as if all strength was seeping out of them. They simply weren't responding to his brain in the normal way, hanging feebly beneath him in the water and constantly going under the lilo – making it impossible to clamber on to it, and forcing him backwards instead.

His upper body and arms still seemed to be holding out – but only just – as if they were rapidly following the deterioration of his lower torso.

He knew he had to get back to the villa – and help. But how, if he could barely move? And who from? Al had told him he'd be out for the day sailing, and he couldn't speak Spanish to either the neighbours or the ambulance service. Moreover, he now doubted he could walk at all, let alone lug himself out of the pool and get to his mobile. Everything suddenly seemed to be shutting down, including every way of escape.

A flood of fear now suddenly overcame him.

'Don't panic,' he told himself. That will only make thing worse. Calm down, and breathe the best you can, Little shallow breaths, not long deep ones. Positive thoughts, not desperate ones. Small, even tiny kicks, to get himself to the steps – only a tantalising few feet away. Surely if this *were* anaphylaxis, you could conquer it if you remained calm?

And indeed this worked for a while, a short while.

But just minutes later he felt a strange tingling and noticed a bright red rash swiftly spreading all over his upper torso, making it look just like a world map, with country after country taking shape. Fascinating, if it hadn't been terrifying.

Now he was barely able to breathe – as if his throat were closing up. Every breath was now becoming shorter than the last, and attempting to make bigger inhalations made the next one shorter still.

Shorter, shorter, shorter, until no more breaths came.

Even in his final terrifying moments, as his hands slipped from the lilo, he was able to reflect on the appalling irony of being brought down not by a massive police force, but by a creature less than half an inch long.

CHAPTER 42

SYDNEY

It had been a scorching day in Sydney, and the news was full of anxieties about the tinder-dry countryside and the danger of fires. Far too hot for Alice to work in the garden, and far too noisy to do so in the house, with the cricket on again at full blast.

But at last it was cooling down. It would now be eight in the morning in England, and Alice was really looking forward to the Skype call arranged with Liz. Nothing like old friends, she thought with pleasurable anticipation.

But suddenly, at the arranged time, an unexpected face came up – that of Robin Marshal. For a worrying moment she feared something might have happened to Pam, extremely relieved when he launched off into small talk. How was she, John, her father, the weather and so on.

And then he changed abruptly.

'Alice, I want to show you something.' He held up an English newspaper to the camera – a tabloid. Its front page was dominated by a huge headline: THE FINAL STING. And underneath was a photograph – old, but instantly recognisable from those in her files. A face she could never forget.

'Yes, it *is* Big Mack', Robin confirmed. 'He's dead.'

'*Dead*? Good God! What happened?

'You're not going to believe this, but he died in a swimming pool – in Spain.'

'*Spain*? I thought he was in Brazil!'

'We all did. Fools, all of us. In fact, I'm feeling really embarrassed about that. We should all have been far more questioning about those threatening letters and planted media stories, rather than jumping to conclusions as we did – especially with my detective background. And Tim's, come to that. Hardly professional.

Anyway, they say he was living a cushy life in the hills above Marbella, no doubt protected by the local British and Spanish mafia, and pretending to be a retired businessman.'

'So he had everyone looking for him in the wrong country.'

'Yes, I'm afraid he did.' Robin heard an audible sigh.

'So he drowned in a swimming pool?'

'No, he actually died from a couple of wasp stings. He almost certainly didn't know he was anaphylactic – as many people don't until it's too late. A pretty nasty death by all accounts, although in this case you could hardly say undeserved.'

Alices's mind shot back to the year before when she was staying with her father in France, and a young girl had been killed by a wasp on a fruit stall in the local market, and nobody had time to react quickly enough – not knowing what was wrong. Who would, until disaster struck?

'Anyway', continued Robin, 'a neighbour happened to spot him floating face down in the pool from his upstairs window. When he went to check, he was covered all over by a red rash, a clear indication of anaphylactic shock. The Spanish doctors confirmed that's what killed him, not drowning. In fact, there was no water in his lungs.

Apparently, he'd been living in a two-villa complex with another chap, also on the run, who was immediately arrested on his return from a day out sailing. It was bloody lucky he didn't find the body – or he'd almost certainly have buried it. In which case none of us would ever have known and the police would have been after him forever. And in bloody Brazil, the wrong country. And even the wrong *continent*, for God's sake.'

He paused for a moment.

'Anyway, there's something else. I called my old police pal, Jim Fawcett, down the coast in Estepona – you know, the chap who helped when Pam and I were attacked. He talked to his Guardia Civil friends, and they told him a couple of things that are pretty frightening. First they found a packed suitcase, a false passport and tickets for that very evening. They were tickets and boarding passes from Malaga to Paris and then the Eurostar train to London.

Then they found maps, and among them was a plan of Bighton – our village. He *was* clearly coming to get us. We can be pretty certain of that, though it's not public knowledge. The rest of the world only has the media stuff. You may even get some news out there in Australia – it's certainly a big enough story here, and the journalists are *relishing* the idea of him being knocked off by an insect, rather than by an international police force.

Ironically, Big Mack may have done the world a last favour – encouraging people to have themselves checked for anaphylaxis before it's too late.'

Alice's mind was racing, initially hugely relieved that she – and others – were no longer under threat, but quickly hauling in a whole host of other implications.

'Anyway, it appears that he seriously wanted to go on with his vendetta against us. At least we've got *our* lives back, now he's lost his.'

There was a long pause before Alice responded, and with an audible sigh.

'So I never needed to come out here at all.'

'Well, you certainly did at the time. You absolutely *couldn't* have gone on watching your back like that. Intolerable!'

Alice sighed. 'I suppose so. But God knows what I'll do now. John loves it here, and so does Dad. They've both settled in like ducks to water. But I have to admit, I'm having second thoughts. And had them even before this call.'

Robin paused, concerned by her tone of voice.

'Give it time, Alice. Remember it's very early days. A big change like that takes a lot of getting used to.'

'Certainly does. Anyway, Robin, many thanks for telling me.'

||||||

It was only after the call ended that Alice realized to her embarrassment that she hadn't even asked after Pam, so profoundly relieved that Big Mack was dead.

'Another gorgeous day!' Her father was suddenly beside her, all smiles.

'Letter for you, darling,' said John, appearing at the door. 'Posted from here.'

'Here? I wonder who it's from.' Alice, for obvious reasons, had been giving her address to very few people.

She tore it open and looked up. 'Gosh, I've passed the first of my exams.'

'Congratulations!' they both chimed in.

'But,' she smiled, tossing the letter on the table, 'that hardly matters now. I've got some other, *really* good news. Mack's dead, so we can all go home!'

She noticed that neither of them smiled back. Suddenly she was locked in fear all over again.

ACKNOWLEDGEMENTS

We would like to thank several people and organisations for their help and advice:

Stuart Bowman, Her Majesty's Prison and Probation Service
Alan Mitchell, formerly Detective Chief Superintendent,
Metropolitan Police, Scotland Yard
The Reverend Jonathan Aitken
Neil Hudson, psychologist
Timothy Ffytche, surgeon
Bruno Olivieri, Mayor of St Hippolyte-du-Fort
Detective Sergeant Andy Warne, Devon and Cornwall Police,
Plymouth
Edward King, Coupe des Nations
Nicola Morrison, Operating Theatre Sister
Parkinson's Disease Society
Anaphylaxis Campaign
The Ritz Restaurant, London
The Lion, Waddesden
Kingston Hospital
Imperial War Museum, Duxford

Liz and Donough – a wife and husband writing team, are the joint authors of the thriller Serial Damage, where we first meet Alice Diamond and Robin Marshal.

Liz Cowley had a long career as an advertising copywriter and Creative Director, working in several of the world's leading agencies. A long-time fan of poetry, she enjoyed success with her first collection, A Red Dress, published in 2008 and her second, What am I Doing Here? (2010), which were then made into a theatrical show – first staged in Dublin, then as the finale of the West Cork Literary Festival and later touring the UK. 'And guess who he was with?' was followed by two popular poetry books for gardeners, Outside in my Dressing Gown, and Gardening in Slippers. A further humorous poetry book, Pass the Prosecco, Darling, all about cooking disasters and other kitchen dramas, was her next collection. She has since co-written a war novel, From One Hell to Another, with ehr husband Donough, as well as a third gardening poetry book, Green Fingers.

Before turning to writing, Donough O'Brien enjoyed a successful marketing career in the US and Europe. His previous books include Fame by Chance, looking at places that became famous by a twist of fate; Banana Skins, covering the slips and screw-ups that brought the famous down to earth; Numeroids, a book of numerical nuggets, and In the Heat of Battle; a study of those who rose to the occasion in warfare and those who didn't. His latest historical book was WHO? The most remarkable people you've never heard of. Donough also co-authored the thriller Peace Breaks Out with the late Robin Hardy, as well as From One Hell to Another, with his wife Liz Cowley, about the role of the Spanish in the French Resistance. Also co-written with Liz is Testosterone, a science fiction novel.

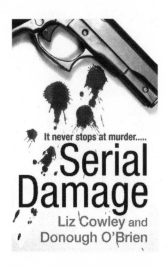

It never stops at murder.....

Serial Damage

Liz Cowley and
Donough O'Brien

A merciless killer with no apparent motive. A series of murders with no discernible pattern. How can he be stopped?

In disconnected locations all over the world a killer plies his terrible trade, seemingly selecting victims at random and killing without remorse. The crimes are the result of one man's obsessive mind, a man warped by a litany of slights and disappointments since childhood for which he seeks methodical and terrible revenge.

Because of the geographical spread of his chilling, 'motiveless' murders, they might normally be impossible to solve, but inexperienced and ambitious police psychologist Alice Diamond may unwittingly hold the dramatic key to his downfall…

A riveting thriller in the best traditions of Barbara Vine, Patricia Highsmith and Val McDermid, Serial Damage will keep you gripped to the very last page.

AVAILABLE FROM AMAZON AND ALL GOOD BOOKSHOPS

URBANE

Urbane Publications is dedicated to
publishing books that challenge, thrill and fascinate.

From page-turning thrillers to literary debuts,
our goal is to publish what
YOU want to read.

Find out more at

urbanepublications.com